The Sylvia Plath Effect

The genius. Diary of the unstable misfit.

Abigail George

Mwanaka Media and Publishing Pvt Ltd,
Chitungwiza Zimbabwe
*
Creativity, Wisdom and Beauty

Publisher: *Mmap*
Mwanaka Media and Publishing Pvt Ltd
24 Svosve Road, Zengeza 1
Chitungwiza Zimbabwe

mwanaka@yahoo.com
mwanaka13@gmail.com
https://www.mmapublishing.org
www.africanbookscollective.com/publishers/mwanaka-media-and-publishing
https://facebook.com/MwanakaMediaAndPublishing/

Distributed in and outside N. America by African Books Collective
orders@africanbookscollective.com
www.africanbookscollective.com

ISBN: 978-1-77933-139-7
EAN: 9781779331397

DISCLAIMER
All views expressed in this publication are those of the author and do not
necessarily reflect the views of *Mmap*.

To Ambrose, Ethan and Rosaline, with intense love

Acknowledgements

A mother's love is everything. Mine carried me through the years that it took to write this book.

I would like to thank my mother for her wit (she has an incredible sense of humour). I would also like to thank her for inimitable style, grace and beauty in everything that she does.

To my dad, for every laugh, tenderhearted moment, for discussions late into the night, for being a shoulder to cry on. For the many years of friendship and private space where secrets were both disclosed and kept.

For my brother, for everything. Thank you, always.

For my nieces and nephews who multiply the love and patience I carry in my heart, thank you.

For my muse, Ambronese *George,* who inspired the chapter *Vanessa Bell, the other genius sister* and who motivates me every day to get out of bed and write.

May your journeys and destinations always be one of beauty.

Grateful, thankful, appreciative.
Gqeberha, 9 March 2024

Table of Contents

Jean Rhys, the unstable genius
Aspects of Dickinson, the poet
Anonymous, the virgin slate
Bessie Head, her alter ego
When you say you don't love me at all
Leonard and Virginia Woolf, the honeymoon
Vanessa Bell, the other genius sister
The curious language of Laura, Lynn and Peter
Dear Husband
Scottie and Zelda Fitzgerald

Introduction note:

There is mind energy in the cycles of life that have become the norm transforming the ways in which we think about indoctrination and religion, thinking and psychopathology, overthinking and psychology, education and neuroscience. In the love/hate relationship we have with the self, the ego, the illusory image that we have with our bodies, something is distorted, misrepresented and misplaced to a certain degree. Self-love is an act which is not engaged with at a basic level of understanding. When we change, when any transformation takes place on the cellular level, physical, biological, psychic, intellectual, mental and emotional there is no movement towards fear, no understanding of the lack of energies or separation anxiety. We as humanity only engage with self-love when we experience relationship. It somehow leaves us satiated. We enter this essential dimension without ego. Only with a brain drained with surrender. Surrender to God, faith, will, discipline and stamina. I understand my own psychological pain. I did not hurt myself as a child. Adults hurt and wounded me very deeply. They left a detailed blueprint upon my consciousness of all the negative traits and characteristics I had. I was stupid, I was not capable of being loved because I was not good enough. Both my parents decided this. I did not finish high school. Both of my siblings went to university. In my early twenties my parents had me certified. I would have been sent to Sterkfontein which was an hour outside of Johannesburg. I was the black sheep of the family. I was labeled a basketcase who could not get her act together and the words "mental" and "sick" were words used to describe my maladjusted personality and my maladaptive behaviour.

As a child, the more I tried to adjust my behaviour around my neglectful and mentally ill mother the more I was punished for it. My childhood and adolescence was difficult and challenging. My younger sister became extraordinarily successful. I knew (instinct told me) that my mother did not love me in the same way she loved my sister and brother. I knew I had to improve my behaviour, my personality, the outline of the borders of my psychological framework but I was only causing more physiological damage to myself. My sister was loved by the same sex parent. My mother motivated her, encouraged her, they participated in rituals like shopping together. My sister has inner peace. She lives in Europe. She is a socialite. I live like a recluse. I am lonely but in my past, present and future loneliness I have found a spiritual perspective on life. I remain prayerful in the silence of the hours. Often there is no one to speak to about my ideas, there is no one to ask me how I am doing and this has all been an authentic choice.

In silence I meditate on nature, solitude and my inward life. The external world around me, my external locus of control and my immediate environment is imperfect. There are days that it shatters my quiet and then fear becomes a choice, my choice. I become fearful of my future. I have never had men, alpha males become aggressive towards me, brutalise or become physical towards me but the emotional pain that I carry stems from my dysfunctional family, from my brother and his girlfriend, my sister and my parents. My mother has never told me that she loves me, I am forty-four years of age now and she has never said that she is proud of me. Her feedback is critical. She devotes herself to my sister. She dotes on my brother. When I had a bipolar relapse and landed at Sunnyside when she came to visit me she would ignore me and speak to the other patients. I have come to

7

accept this behaviour from my family. I don't become emotional. My tears would only make them mimic me.

Everything has life and an innate ability for growth. In the case of an individual, life guides the overachiever to success and personal development, the weighing down of stress and negativity and the lightness of inner peace. When I think of the lightness of inner peace I think of redemptive love and salvation. The believing in and of a higher power and being a practising Christian for most of my life has led me through to a warped pleasure and pain time cycle. This source has often led me to conflict. Oftentimes I haven't been able to overcome my problems and depressive, manic and hypomanic episodes within my family. I have turned to books on self-help and how to improve myself. Sometimes my behaviour has improved when I am in an environment that benefits me, where there are advantages for my personal growth and fulfillment, when there are gaps for me to become empowered and uplifted.

The phantom for me is my uneasiness in crowds, disharmony within myself and that that is rooted in the family nucleus and dynamic, the inertia that existed within my insomnia and chronic fatigue, the near fatal relapse after a recovery after episodic bipolar. When I was at Provincial Hospital (certified by my mother who did not trust my then boyfriend's intentions towards me at the time) I had a brief glimpse inside myself. My mother was right and I was wrong. I became suicidal and was aggressive towards the other young women in the ward. I was placed in an isolation booth for two months. I was later diagnosed with covid. When I was released I lost the love of my life (I told myself he would be understanding of the situation but he broke up with me via text message). I became stronger as the weeks went by and began to understand what exactly purity meant as time went by. Sexual purity, ritualistic purification and the dimensions of light in a prodigal vessel.

I am in my forties with still so much to learn about the psychology of the brain. I am a work in progress trying to improve my physical and mental health, the relationships within my family and I am learning not to engage with my siblings (although this has been difficult since they are demanding of my attention, my time and they are very consistent with this). When my parents ignore me my world falls apart. I feel they did not give me the tools, or teach me coping skills, how to deal with men who make inappropriate or lewd comments, who try to force their company and conversation upon me. I have this mental picture of myself that I have to calm down in order for me to interact with other minds of either gender.

My inner power has a poetic force. I have experienced hardship and despair, suffering and the malevolence of others towards me. The world leader Nelson Mandela said that it always seems impossible until it is done. I volunteer, I strive to donate goods, shoes and secondhand clothes and I hand out sandwiches and coffee and have found my purpose. To be kind to others but most of all to myself.

Jean Rhys, the unstable genius

I can hear his voice in my veins. He calls me his, 'Porcelain-darling'. Sometimes in my flat here in London, I would move from one room to the next astonished at this 'love-experiment' I was delving into. I was now once again 'a work in progress' as I had been as a child in Dominica. The first man I ever loved made me feel more of an exile on these London streets. Far away from home, the only home I had ever known. It was the known. Love is like plasma, floating mitochondria, atomic particles, the accurate building up of ignorance into life experience, the harsh, neon underground bricks of illness. Love for me was always an unlikely dilemma. Do I, or don't I? Sometimes I think we live with ghosts. Love is a ghost. It is ancient as illness but it makes me bleed at the starting line. Curtains at the open window of the hotel room are moving in sync with my little bleeding scarlet heart. Why do I write? I want to find myself in eternity when I'm in heaven. Everything has returned to normal. I am on my own again. I don't want to strike it rich or land me a guy to marry me (both at the same time would be a dream). There will be no reunions with family, with lovers, with 'him', that kind, sincere wealthy man I first met when I was such an ingénue. He taught me the difference between the words, 'authentic', 'squalor', 'but these are terrible living conditions', and 'you can even find human nature in a symphony if you listen close enough'. He taught me the meaning of words like, 'the brittle movements and accurate moments of solitude', 'how to be astonished at how ignorant people were, how vain women and men were', 'all pictures always carried powerful observations of life in the details'. I would hear his voice everywhere I went in the beginning stages of our relationship (I called our little affair). His voice healed some parts of me especially when the dark air of night was advancing. 'God is mostly in your head but most people do what their hearts tell them to do.' 'Life is boring and we need activities like love to get us through the day. We're a match. People think life owes them something if they're not born rich but even rich people are lonely and ignorant. They can go to the best schools in the world, but are they educated, no, cultured, no. Have you ever felt abandoned, neglected, ill at the thought of being rejected (I felt like that my whole childhood) I wanted to ask but was too afraid to, too afraid he would think I was a mouse, weak. There was clarity in that. You need to think more of yourself, Jean love. You need to express yourself. If you feel indignant, feel indignant. If you feel confident, feel confident. Don't be so afraid of the world around. What is the worst thing that could happen (I already knew, that someone could laugh in my face, stare me down until I looked away but I never confided this in him because there was no reason to)? Sometimes I think you feel terribly lost. I see a terror in your eyes as we leave one another. You remind me of a lotus flower and for me it is the most beautiful flower in the world. He could articulate it (love), show it, examples of it (I could only describe it, make plans for it for the most part in my head, connecting threads of the purest thoughts of it in black notebooks). I was his pretty doll whom he spoke of in whispers to in the dark. Jean, sometimes I think you are hiding something away from me. I think an entire wonderland must exist inside your head for your own pleasure. What sweetness that must come with. It must taste refreshing. It must taste like pink happiness, a deposit of charm in a room that has not felt it for days, for my Jean, my bird without wings. And so, his champagne voice would carry me through the day and for most of the night for this insomniac. Sometimes I could feel the stress on my heart, its thudding, hammering away pressure and there was nothing in the world I could do about it. All I had to do was to live. I would watch children sometimes and think to myself what their gifts to the world would be when they grew up. Sometimes my heart would turn to paste as I watched them and I would think that now, finally everything had been taken away from me. I could never be free and then I would walk down back streets. There would always be an undeniable lightness in the road's blackness as evening began to settle all around me. Its magical fingers in my hair, the wind rearranging my hat, massaging thoughts of rope and poison, putting stones into the pockets of my coat and walking into a lake filled with ice and trees at the bottom into my mind's eye. I would think of the dilemma that faced Romeo and Juliet and how sometimes when I was feeling very low, how that same dilemma faced me. I wanted to be myself but not on my own like this. I knew I had failed. I did not know how to get back to life. I did not know how to dance to modern society's beat. I did not know what modern meant anyway but I knew I was a most modern woman attached to absolutely nobody and nothing. And then the tears would come streaming down my face. I could not stop them and why I. Life would have not been fair to me. I did not know anything about modern acrobatics and the flying trapeze artist was a comic to me and sometimes my mind's eye was a width of a thread and it was simply connected to nothing. Some days I would feel brave as I if I had a destination in my step but I knew that was a lie. Soon everywhere I went I would hear his voice in my head, as if he was with me in the room. 'You can survive anything, Jean as long as you put your heart and mind to it. You look beautiful tonight, simply divine, and come here let me hold you. It feels as if it's been forever since I've last seen you.' By that time, he was already a ghost. It didn't feel real to me. His voice had no substance but it kept me company, the illusion was so strong. I didn't know how to distance myself away from that habitat of his beautiful house filled with fireplaces, flowers and pictures hanging on the walls of landscapes, a wine cellar. I just wanted to dissolve. Sometimes you live poverty. I've lived in poverty. And at first, I didn't want people to see me like that. You know, drab, pathetic, old clothes, out of fashion. Funny, but it made a difference to them, made their hearts and their diplomatic hearts and heads softer towards me. They exhibited empathy to what I always thought was my unlikely demise. They gave me money and I would use it to live as best I could. There was an understanding. Out of sight, out of mind. It was fine if I was going out of my mine with loneliness so long as it was on their terms. And when a guy (I really don't really his name, how we met), he finally he broke off the affair a few months later, he was very diplomatic and suave about it. Although I couldn't understand how he could be so composed about the whole deal. To them money meant success. I had no money. I wished sometimes that I could distance myself away from it, my love for it but I needed to live like other people did, don't you see. Whatever that word 'normal' meant it gave me Goosebumps just thinking about it. And then in the end I thought it was normal to distance myself from society. From London to Paris, Europe, what a pilgrimage, what a privilege. Whoever gets the chance to travel these days? And then I was soon back in London again. Whatever happened in Paris had been an adventure but now it was over. Sometimes I felt vertigo as I was walking on those London streets. I felt blessed with the knowledge that somehow, I was perhaps writing for a generation that would come years after me in a golden age. It was a generation who was now experiencing life as children while I was a grown woman. Sometimes I thought to myself I was not meant for this world. In the evenings London would become a ghost nation but I did not want to be stuck in a room. It was too depressing. I became too aware of my current situation. It would make me feel sad.

I would feel like having a drink and then my whole outlook on life would change after I had the drink within me. The man who lived below me would knock a broom into his ceiling and ask me to 'keep it down in there' (whatever the hell that meant). I didn't know what on earth I got up to in the early hours of the morning. Sometimes I thought I would just be writing, scribbling away, staring at the walls. I would think about love, how much I really liked the idea of it. There are a lot of things in this world that are rotten, unpleasant things to deal with. In the evening or usually when I am alone something always seems to loose itself violently from me. Sadness, a wounded feeling as if I almost don't belong in this world and in a way, I know I don't fit. Perhaps I am too reckless in the choices that I make. Perhaps I am not a safe person to be around. Too much of a thinker, brooder, reader always keeping love and the attraction of it in the dark until I can feel pin points of lights trying to break through the cracks. I am no good. I am bad at love. I am bad at affairs and matters of the heart and bad at relationships. I must rest now. Tomorrow is another day. So, I wait until the room is filled with darkness and I listen to the noises in the street outside, downstairs, in my own room. And I know I've walked that street today like a ghost as if I was not aware of my surroundings. Soup is always good for the soul, as are confessions. Here is one for one. I don't believe in the death of things anymore. I believe in life as much as that is hard to believe. If only someone knew me well. If only I had a companion. If only I didn't have to suffer for my art. All of my life I watched women in their relationships with men. How they would smile, turn their head, their eyes watchful and waiting, how they would smooth their hair down, arrange the food, the salad on the plate or cast their eyes over a menu and how the men were pensive, eager to please in this sunny environment. How could I have known then as a child that I was not one of them? And that I was never going to grow up and be one of them? I would watch these women always smiling; listening (but were they really listening). And I wondered why these women with their fine clothes, elaborate hats, and brooches, why never spoke back. They were always nodding their heads like puppets. I knew from an early age I was not too pretty so I would have to work hard, but also I would have to discipline myself not to be too smart. I reckoned that people's lives are meant to be celebrated when they're alive, not dead. There was always something pure about the day as I set about my walk and there is something to be celebrated in that. The union of life mixed with the elixir of what I drank (and I always thought of it as an elixir). I was not built like that, to be tough I mean. I was never meant to be a bully or a tyrant. I just did not have that warmth in my voice, that kind of spirit flowing in my blood. If poetry is an elixir then prose is food for thought. I've walked past people and they've stared at me. I've looked away but sometimes when I really think of getting to grips with the situation, I want them to try and understand me so I stare back. What do they see, a casualty disconnected from the rest of the world? I live so simply. My life is easy and cheap. My supper is usually bread and cheese. It is always bread and cheese. No change there and my hands smell like soap and this room's bare bones creak under my stockinged feet at night. Writing has become my ritual. It has become my escape from grief and raw anguish and frustration. Sometimes the process of writing torments me but I also feel very anchored by it. It's therapeutic, it minimises the stress that I feel thudding inside my head and it gives me a sense of purpose. All the words seduce me, gets under my skin. It is so intense, this pleasure that unravels and seems to release the chill out of me on cold nights. But I can no longer feel the weight of the world resting on my shoulders so acutely. The words seem to paint that blue pearl into a rainbow of magic colour. Into childlike stuff of

15

fairies, dust, a water wonderland, into soul and life, everything of beauty and not a disturbing sense of things. I always wished as a child to make contact with things like that, magical things. I'm thirsty so I get up for some water. I can still taste the salt in the air coming in from the sea in Dominica. Why would I go back? Sometimes I remember why and sometimes I don't. Fast forward to a flat in London and I go by the name now of Jean Rhys. A name I have changed so many times. I have no money, no skills, and no form of employment. The cheques come in regularly. He called me a 'porcelain darling', 'daring good girl', 'special' and that I was 'loveliness personified'. He had kind eyes. He was so authentic and a real gentleman. I mean authentic in the terms of he was a man who was made of substance and everything around him, his home, his household, his wealth felt real to me as I entered the foyer and stared at the flowers in the vase that seemed to welcome even me. I believed nothing was wrong and even when the affair ended I still thought perhaps there would be contact again and even a friendship but years have passed (the poet in me I guess came up with these foolish notions). Realising that the past is past even the temporary frightened me to death. But there had to have been some reward, something golden that I could get out of the equation of knowing this man and coming into his world even for a short period of time. I could not solely have duped myself into thinking, into believing that it was just a lark on his part. You know that whole easy situation. I could think about these things for hours on end, fill my entire day on the he said she said transmission of our conversations. Sometimes I would get stuck on a sentence, just the tone, how he would express himself and it would drive me crazy, up the wall and I would will my brain to dissolve it. It would feel brutal but brutality in the end also serves its own purpose. It will make you realise that you need to rest. I don't know quite when I've finished with something.

When I have to quit it but I do know when I have to rest. When I'm kaput. I'm too young to know about those sorts of things, that's what I wanted to say at the time. I was thinking it all the time watching the creases in the corners of his mouth. How the fleshy part of the skin in the middle of his forehead was crinkling up as he watched my reaction. I know he was just testing me to see if I would fly out of control, would she make a scene? How would the past few months come to an end? I felt like an orphan. I shouldn't say things like that but that is what I felt like. Lost, terribly afraid of the world, neglected, abandoned, no home, no name and family. There was no hope in damned hell to resurrect my lone self. There were parts of me that were wolfish, that was the part of me that could fight, battle (I have the scars to prove it) if I had to. No, if I was challenged. But I also withdrew easily and that was the weakest part of me. It didn't matter what kind of climate I found myself sheltered by. I embraced skating on illness and when I did, I yearned the most for my art and all my little rituals. Now I am tired of the years of cold I have lived through and this incessant hunger that I feel for attention and most of all my neediness. Violets were my favourite flowers in the world. Maybe because they're so pretty and cheerful they make me feel that way. They don't make me feel like death, volcano dust or blue warmed up. Sometimes I dream of my mother's fingers knitting, not braiding my hair. In the middle of the night I come upon a sleeping world, a dream world. I journey there for a while pacing back and forth, sometimes crying, sometimes in a sombre mood before I fall asleep myself. The stars are like birds in my eyes on the nights you can see stars in London. They are like birds with their wings outstretched. Ready to meet the oncoming edge of the sky or a sword of air. All 'Ella' had was imagination and she kept that close to her. 'Ella' was always secretive and I have kept that because if I didn't I would have come undone a long time ago. I am what I am because I have wanted people to believe it, especially other women. In life there are always choices, pleasure, desires. I always kept waiting for love to change everything. A Prince charming and as dark as an Arabian knight in shining armour to rescue me. But life never goes according to plan although I am an open door. Sometimes it feels as if I come alive in the dark. The sun is like a mirror. If it's there I never see it. I am not conscious of its light, and my reflection in it. I can feel (I've always been aware of this for what feels like forever) the dark side of life more intensely than the lighter side of life, of it. My hair was not spun gold. It was dark. I did not believe in fairies and their wings or that Dominica was an island but I did like the trees. They were my favourite and the open fields and when a spell of tiredness came upon me, when I couldn't breathe because of the heat I would imagine. My goal became to fall in love with warriors in suits who had wonder guts in their blood. I've loved many and I've lost some along the way. Splendid confidantes that I held in high esteem as if royalty. I've learned to go on loving although it is the hard way. You go on paying the price one too many times. There's a flaw in passion, a conspiracy in love, that hate that always cornered me on the playing fields of childhood that seemed to flow my way as a gauche chorus girl. You know once upon a time there was a man who wanted to adopt me. I think he wanted to take care of me and be a fatherly figure. Some kind of mentor, a friendly man who would keep me out of the firing line of the inquiring gazes of others who would exchange company for money. One last time I am more in love with being in love than anything else. The air is crisp (a tattoo on the green landscape). It feels as if I am living in an ancient world collapsing under meteors. What does progress mean to a writer? Write more books but they have to have a market and they have to sell well but the writer must always be morose and depressed. Very difficult when it comes to giving interviews. I do not know what impact my books have on the rest of the world and I would like it to stay that way. I know that human behaviour is predictable. It is also a precious cargo. But I am made of glass. Why call off the splendid search (such an adventure) for the adventurous spirit at heart, that instinct. I am the feminine lark, the songbird. In my line of work there is such a thing as clarity but no such things as clocks. What is the meaning of that four-letter word l-o-v-e? And when it is nailed to my heart why do I stammer when I speak, why does my heart beat to another rhythm, cadence (I can hear it as if it has gone underground somewhere). I have to mine it like a mineral deposit. In love when I have fallen, fallen hard all my thoughts are hushed up, meshed together mystically. It is hard for me to understand men sometimes, to have a concept of them as an object, to understand their failure to communicate and the world they inhabit, their domain. The sense of their beliefs and mine differs profoundly. They can be monsters made of winter, coldly inspiring all kinds of aches and pains of the mental kind, cerebral but they can alo be incredibly vulnerable. I ask myself, do I want to write. I can't remember when I wanted or started to write. When I received that inclination from the universe. I only knew that I had to write to save myself. I don't remember when I remedied the thought of not dreaming with drinking. Alcoholism and crazy seemed inseparable and here is when the writing comes in, rescues me. The writing was always a useful exercise. I never learned to smile those early years in London, never believed I was a rose among the thorns. Perhaps all young women are supposed to think like that (that is what drives them, for the better part of my adult life it haunted me) and made me feel insecure in the bloom of their first love affair. I was not a flower, could not wrap my words around the tones of crisp English. But I remember the tears. As a child the back of my throat is a land of thirst. I knew that there was something else out there for me.

Something besides the loneliness, the sadness and despair that I sometimes fell into, that became my child's mind-sanctuary. Dampness seeps into the lining of my coat. There are flecks of cloud in the blue sky. But is it enough to want desire? The faded grass under the leaves, under my shoes. The faded grass under autumn leaves, Whitman's leaves of grass and the sacred contract that existed between human nature and nature. The woman in the park she will not appear the same in a photograph as she will in memory. This Eve taken from Adam's rib who was a daughter doing what her mother did. Woman, the ethereal girl figure turning on a pedestal with her eye on the prize of love. I have my observations of them, these others, glorified futuristic poster girls for motherhood (who would in a few years' time settle down for life). They will live as they dream in their sleep and dream to live. And all my life I have wondered what do children communicate when they laugh? Turkish slippers small enough for small frail bird feet, a gift from a friend. A draft of sunlight in the air burns bright. I am held, caught up in its grasp. Illness has touched the glinting, sharp parts of me. It is not the bag of bones why have you forsaken me, my skull, my frame, celestial nimble fingers, and patella. You centre of my being, nerve, every fibre of my being, brain, heart of mine, platelet, aorta, and corpuscle. Why this unfinished prophecy? And then it grew cold. It is as if cosmic force was holding all those clouds up together. The world around me, its people, and the rich became wealthier, girls on the chorus line retired from the theatre life when they got married and everything around me moved forward. It got its talons in me and I never became that selfless kind of person I wanted to be. Darkness falls. At my core lies gravity. All my life I have wanted to be beautiful. I have everything else. I will never get married. It is all becoming a bit too much for me. A bit of losing my mind, my heavy head giving way. I can't keep lying. Keeping on and on with it. I must be honest. I must be truthful. The unopened bottle of gin is there on the table. I must stop wasting my time. I must be brave and throw my head back and love, laugh in the face of adversity. I must stop wasting time. If I don't eat something I will disappear, that superimposed elusive part of me, the soul, the frightened part, and the physical and private body of the subconscious. I am becoming a non-entity. I can become used to the idea that I do not exist in the material world where the others meet. Men and woman of similar interests and backgrounds and who have common goals, that connects them to each other. The morning air in my room is cold, heavy and still. So I make way to the kitchen to smoke and although there are rats in the ceiling it is not all doom and gloom. The writing life has chosen me. Being happy is a unique state of mind. I can remember when I felt as if I was let loose on the world off the ship from Dominica to go to school in England. If only I knew then what I know now. London wasn't a distant place, it was a distant planet. The results can be electric when opposites attract. I could dance but I was not good enough, not graceful, less than the other girls. I could act a little but then there was my West Indian accent. So, in the end it was decided that I was a terrible actress. I could not cry on command in class instead I started to laugh and to laugh and to laugh and that drew attention to myself. An artist works with materials at hand. Voice, the life force of the body, touch, hand movement, eye coordination, physical body, and the senses. What can be more precious than to be coloured by an auspicious space and when the abundant universe gives you wings? To start from (childhood) and to transition it from a dream (to act on the stage) to a comfort zone (ending up in the chorus). Sharp, blistering, in a brutal dissolve came the comments when I was younger living in a house with other siblings, a father for a doctor and a mother who was always certain that I would fail if I set my heart on anything. Threads, connected by them govern us as we are by the books we read. I have a theory about books. In the long run they will make you wiser but they will also make you cry, laugh, as wise as an owl. Deep unhappiness can be challenging, that and learning to fight your battles. What many people don't realise is that egocentrism can be good for you up to a certain extent. Especially when you are given a stage, an expectant audience (a waiting one). When you are expected to shine brilliantly. It is egocentrism that wants, drives you and that gives you the ability to do well (ambition), expect a rousing applause, admiration, adoration, a standing ovation and to a certain extent love and acceptance and your abilities for being recognised for what they are. Why is simply achieving happiness so hard? The negative ruins optimism. It ruins me for good. When I was younger, just a slip of a girl I wondered what having a backbone meant. My first prince did not love me. The most that he could give of himself was never quite enough. I wonder if the vegetarian restaurant that I frequented when I lived in London is still open. I ate the noodles and the soup it floated in heartily while watching the world go by. In those early years I was afraid of what was going to happen to me. Would I ever make it? Would the lady in me ever come out, deserving of love, out of the hole, the void? This scared cat. I'm frightened of people who constantly tell you that they love you. Truth and beauty exists in a microcosm of things. Scientists will say it is atoms while I say I am a voyager and these are the sum of my parts. I believe in having interests and sticking to them. Having goals sometimes gives me light-headed feeling. Is that what I am really supposed to be here for? It makes me feel locked up, as if I have to have a witness or witnesses for everything that I do and envisage for my life. I am always struck by how unsure I was by the cruel wonders, how filled with dangers the world was once. I did not become immune to it quickly. Do I have my upbringing to thank for that, I do not know. I feel lost sometimes when I stare at my reflection put out by unwanted visitors who go from door-to-door but I also feel pure of heart too. Men have done me no wrong, that charade is long gone. It is I who have been foolish and reckless with my own heart. You see why blame them. I miss the sea and the view from the top of the hill in Dominica. The horses we had when I was growing up and when I got on that boat with my aunt that day to say goodbye to the world I grew up with forever I asked myself, what would I do in the world? Would I always be petrified, would warmth or the cold always strike me? I was always the curator of wish-fulfilment, dreams, an odd sort of museum where nothing fit because there was no culture to, and no sanctuary. There were moments in childhood when I despaired not having anyone to talk to. I remember the sadness that seemed to pale everything else in comparison. I wanted to be happy but I didn't know why I wasn't a happy child. Why I never smiled like the other girls? I must have been too quiet. I must have been a mute. I must have been a dark mute with a dark soul, intense and always burning rough around the edges. No, I was never like the others. Not like my sisters with their lovely faces. I am not perfect. The perfect partner, co-conspirator, somebody's wife, the perfect daughter, and sister. In the end it is just a not too long list of words. I never wanted to be alone. I did not want to navigate the world flying solo with fingertips caressing maps. I will never forget Paris. I will never forget that I lost a child there and had a daughter. I am a mother, a writer and perhaps I wasn't a very good wife. Of course I went back to Dominica but it wasn't the same. I was older and London had changed me for good. And perhaps it was the snow. I could never get used to the cold you know. The fires that always had to burn (what a waste of fuel) and I never really took care of myself in London the way I did after I got married for the first time, second and third. After the third one I had money from the writing part of my life. Past is past but it was on a certain level it was never quite for me. I distilled it with my pen. Childhood wounded me. It still seeped into me somehow. Through my clothes and it got to the very heart of lonely me. At one point I must have looked like a bird, as thin as one. London wounded me, as did relationships, insights into the observations of other lonely people around me (I would watch them through the window at that vegetarian restaurant or sitting around me at the other tables). Tiredness that crept into my voice. And then later my spirit. I was always ready to fly off the handle. When will the world begin to become fascinating to my bright eyes, my bright intellect? When will I become fierce? I was an extra in the movies once but in the end it did not count for anything. It did not turn into anything. I was still the same old same boring me. And I cried. I would write into the night and I would cry when the rest of the world was sleeping and dreaming or coming out of a club into the empty London streets. And in the morning when I woke up with the rest of the world I felt complete in a way I cannot fully come to grips with or make you understand. And now after all this time that has passed me by, I feel ethereal. I have faced the angelic. It has taken me on and I have won. I am otherworldly by design. A design not of my own making. It has taken years. There is always a lesson in love even though you may think for now it is wounding your spirit. I was a bride. There I said it. There was never a word for this pent–up sadness that sometimes felt poetic. I just knew I was on edge for some reason. I could never be the mistress of this bright and new force within me. Freedom like any consciousness- thinking awareness is a psychological construct. It is nothing more than that and if we think it is going to be more, we are going to be sadly mistaken in the end or we will realise it too late. I was once a daughter then an orphan. I had the maternal instinct in my genes. It had to have been there. To know that kind of love and be on the receiving end of it anchored me. When I held my daughter in my arms I had never felt more at peace with myself. My daughter's childhood songs, her many sweet, curious, inventive faces, the avalanche of presents I bestowed upon her on birthdays and Christmases. She had a father and that was also in a way a gift from me to her in a way even though the three of us couldn't be together, live together properly as a family. She was beautifully well brought up. When do routes become important? I fear only in later life. When you are too set in your ways. When my dear, you are old and think you are going crazy. What would it have been like to watch the Dominican sun setting in a sea lock-and-struggle? I would have given anything to see that tonight. When you're in your bed at night with the thick covers pulled up around you and think you can hear something in the kitchen (when it is only a window you left open or a cupboard door that refuses even with the wind to bang shut). When you think that someone in the dark is out to get you, the bogeyman. I've journeyed. I've journeyed and have no regrets. The living keep on living while the dead turn to dust. Nothing really belongs to us. When we leave this world we take with us the possessions we arrived with – the lone self. Beyond evening's contours are the stars and even further out there is the moon. And if I close my eyes, I can imagine being aware of nature in or touching the sky. I already said I was a bride. But I cannot remember if I felt passion that day. Of course, a ring did mean that now the two of us were now bonded together for life and that was with my first marriage. I had a passion for libraries that mildew smell, the ancient pages that almost seemed to wilt in your hand; those lose pages that seemed to have come undone. I had a passion for books, above all for notebooks I could scribble in to my heart's content, and I always loved to read. How do you shine if you are not guided by 'other hands' and by those 'elders' who had come before you in the world? Pain of the mind can be more devastating, felt more acutely than pain of the body.

In my life there was always the baby, the sister, another sibling has taken my place and now overshadowed me in everything I did. How do you know you're alive? You find poetry, the way of the writer with all the cleansing rituals in the space of the writer, the table, the chair and water to drink, bread and cheese for a meal. And slowly I slip into a routine. I get up in the morning. I smoke. I brush my dishevelled hair. I go for a long walk in the streets of London. I am not yet that famous writer who is now elderly, famous-enough to have a driver to take me around town and pick up parcels before he drops me off at home at a small cottage in Devonshire. And after my walk I must write. I confess. I had a cat once. It was a proper Persian kitten but the people who looked after it didn't look after it really well. The poor thing died of neglect. And then I was sad again for a long time. You have to have a heart to get yourself attached to animals. This is my voice, made of gossamer, tasting like the season's fruits or cauldron (take your pick). It is a voice that sounds like Keats, and I am offering it to the world. It is I who have closed doors on myself, escaped through the window that was left ajar and not the other way around. And these are the notes from a writer's journal, my notes. Shut the door. Shut out the quiet light. Tell yourself to swim away from the tigers with arms pillars of smoke. One day I will find myself in a forest without men, without huntsmen and warriors, nomads and ghosts that burn all hours of the day and night. One day I will dazzle and fizz like a champagne virgin (hiss like a cobra). I will laugh in all their faces. I will weave and thread stories, braid hair and dwell in possibility. My mother taught me that. White Knight you jewel. The bluish sky falls off you. I prefer the word 'solitude' to 'loneliness'. White Knight you jewel of Hollywood. One day I will shut the door. One day I will shut out the quiet light. One day I will tell myself to swim away from the tigers. My tingling arms pillars of smoke. What a pale and beautiful creature you are (you once were upon a time now worlds apart) but are you happy? You went on to paradise and wrote and wrote and wrote and won prizes and planted flags. My beautiful creature as cold as all things that come from the sea, the lover of love and picture of health. I have bits and pieces in memory of you of other peoples' keepsake stuff. The mouth so angelic and so grateful to be kissed and the eyes like dew. I knew at the end of it you would still have a soul to come home to. Alas the same could not be said of me, dude in black, cowboy in black. To yearn for love, to live in that paradise again and again and again is a wish granted to a chosen few, the chosen ones and what happens to the others? The others live to exist for their families, raising their children or for themselves, for their ego. If there is no love to feed you, nurture you, caress your tired or grief-stricken face at the end of the day then I imagine that there are people out there who sometimes feel as lost as I do. What can loneliness communicate to you? It is a lovely feeling. You're freer in a way than other people are. But who is there for you to talk to at the end of the day? People need companions. People need friends and family, loved ones and acquaintances. People need contact, closure, and relationships. There are people who build empires on these kinds of things. And then there are people who need, want, desire love as wide as river, as deep and beautiful as the Pacific. And then there are people who turn their back on that and embrace a life guided by the pulse that tells them to be brave. And to turn their back on a world that calls them an Outsider, a loner, strange with strange ways of doing things, a strange way of thinking. And you just have to have the courage of your convictions if you are this sort of person. I am this sort of person. So weirdly out of sync with the rhythm of other women my age. So good am I at this thing, this sly-odd movement that I have won prizes for it. It feels like a bird's wing in spasm in the air. It feels like a rush of warm, sweet air into the beautiful red ribbons of your heart, a cry in the dark, a promise that you make to meet up with someone in heaven at a deathbed. Someone dear and truly loved who has passed on from this world into the hereafter. What's eternity anyway? A more novel, adventurous dimension because it becomes lovely when you think of it in that way. Not meeting up with strangers but meeting up with familiar faces. The faces that you knew, loved and cherished since birth. They were people who were always a part of your world in one way or another. So I say one day we'll all meet in heaven. We'll make our way there from all of our other destinations that we 'lost' a little self, worth and identity in. Everybody is married in some way to his or her soul and every bit of our soul is intended for and to be hitched, hooked, stitched to God. Whether you want to believe that or not is entirely up to you but to me it makes sense. I love the useful wonder in thinking that. And then there are those lukewarm questions that tug at the puppet strings of the heart. Not floating suspended by nothing but an existential breeze in the air, not drowning just there, behaving mysteriously as if they had all the right in the universe to be there. When I was in love I wanted to know everything about him and nothing at the same time. Falling in love, head over heels, sweeping flaws under the carpet did not come with instructions. I did not know how to correct something I did wrong. Everything was new and pretty. To love someone since you were a child is a very long time. Illusions, they do not come with flaws and they cannot love. They're too much in love with themselves. People do not ask, 'What were you like in the womb?' Men do not say with a great amount of insight, 'You seem to have been a fish with the spirit of a lioness even then.' They're answers for the volcano dreamer. The last battle was always touch and the solution for me is this. My sister and I had a conversation and it went something like this. We ended up not really saying anything at all like most of our conversations these days. God can keep your soul. Let me bury you there in paradise. In no particular place in paradise. In your claustrophobic world where you were so cold. You white knight death cutie on parade. It's the little deaths in pixels from childhood that is as nutritious and forgetful as dreaming. These days everything is crisper. Images are sharper and brighter. (And now what about the men). Of course the men are in secret code so they can never be discovered out. In a mirror I see a wife (always a fretful wife with screaming, crying babies). 'Poor babies,' I enjoyed saying and why didn't he love his beautiful wife more and why was I the chosen one. I couldn't really see why inexperience was so sexy. There is nothing barren about this man's ego. But his hands always felt cold. He had dark, dark hands; skin like velvet and even his eyes were dark. They were always so full of concern for me. I pretended it was wonder. Living your life and moving forward is the easy part. It is the forgetting that is the hardest. I can put a face to a name, city, and occupation. I remember. It is all in the details. I don't want to meet these men in heaven or in any place else. The men with all that sadness, rage and perfect-wonder in their eyes. All their faces look the same to me and after all this time I did not step back from the picture and say I forgive this and I forget that. They look at me as if to say, 'You too had a role in this. A part to play in all that drama.' The drama felt quite useless to me on the one hand and like jazz on the other. 'You're quite mad, you know.' One man told me but he couldn't exactly look me in the eye. So I bravely posed in mask after mask after mask. Another man preferred 'the girl'. Well, that was his thing. He didn't want educated, intelligent or smart. He didn't want cute. He wanted 'the girl'. He wanted a pure, angelic face in beautiful clothes. He wanted obedience. He wanted to be put on a pedestal and worshipped. And so, I did all that. I couldn't quite understand why because I could make conversation but he never wanted to talk and understand how claustrophobic I felt sometimes just being in his presence. It felt completely otherworldly to me. These things called love or rather, 'the affair'. It didn't exactly feel like romance to me. No, there was nothing romantic about it. I feel a great deal of shame because I did not listen to my heart. A heart that was telling me his wife meant a great deal more to him than I did and even on a certain primeval level his wife's body meant a great deal more to him. She had given him children. And he had built the house they all lived in (the one, big, happy and boisterous family). But since this is my secret diary it is just between you and me and nobody else has to know especially my father. I don't want him to think differently about me and the life I chose to give or take a few years ago because I am not that person anymore. And I don't believe that time heals. When people say that it is as if there's something specific to time. There's nothing specific about time and even clarity doesn't even figure into it. I can ask my ancestors why I've never been lucky in love. Why I've failed so dismally in that department (much too much of a daddy's girl)? I can say I will never give my heart away again but I don't believe that. I usually fall in love up to three times a day. I was just starting to feel hungry. And when I am hungry I have my breakfast, usually toast with a smidgen of butter (from a brick that's been standing out on the kitchen table or counter since the following night) or margarine. And I make myself some tea. Just toast (brown bread toasted in the oven like in the old days and I smile when I think to myself that I am from the old days now). I wake up earlier and earlier and go to bed later and later. It feels good to be thirty-two. I didn't feel it (old, stale, as if I was coming into a rut, the state of the nation, the world my generation found themselves in) when it was my birthday but now that the next one is around the corner I am feeling it. It feels like too much effort this morning to make an egg, boiled, fried, or scrambled into bits. So, I'll have my toast with jam this morning. I think of him and everyday it doesn't hurt less, it hurts more. I've given up on humanity. What I see on the news or the little I read in the newspapers terrifies me. It scares me half to death. Children raping children (aren't they just babies), the desolation of poverty and how it isolates people from the mainstream of society. What is relevant to me in society is not relevant to the media. They write what sells and it is usually salacious material. Here today, gone tomorrow or the next week until it comes back as an update or haunts you when you least expect it. It is funny how the mind can play tricks on you especially when you're over thirty, reaching that point of middle age. The news often pins down the status of refugees, painting the women with their children, food aid flown in from abroad, white tent after white tent in a field of white tents and again there are stories of rape and mutilation. It never seems to end. We are capable of many, many things. God can keep you soul and man will take and take everything else. I never thought of myself as a fierce person as a child. I was an introvert. I never thought of my mother as a bully although she could be quite fierce. When I was in London I hid all my diaries at the bottom of my suitcase and forgot about them. In London I would meet a man. We would eat noodles at a restaurant or go out for a drink. In Paris life was different. When I would meet a man there we would go out for a drink at a café. The lifestyle in Paris was like that. Drinking sparkling wine into the early hours of the morning. I would become a different person. I liked myself more. When I was with a man I told myself this was it. This is what passion felt like when I was in his arms. This was love, beauty and when it ended, when we went our separate ways there were days when I felt I was going out of my mind. The loneliness, the fear that I would never have that again made me turn to writing. I would open up the black scribbler. I would sit and think to myself isn't that the most perfect word in the universe. In the middle of the night in my stockinged feet I would just glance out of my window and watch the world go by, trembling, chilled to the bone, drinking milk from a chipped mug. And I would write and write and write. It would simply pour out of me like rain from the sky while I would sit in my room. And so a book would turn into the pages of books, a stream of thought would lead to a threshold. I could now connect threads from my past to my present. I could still remember the ice house of my childhood, aunts, visitors to the house, voices, a mother who did not have the heart, the slightest idea, nor inclination to love me. She could murder chickens though. Strangle them by their necks. In a way she strangled me too. Perhaps when life is hard for women when they are girls who always have to compete for the love of their father that kind of intent is simply woven into their consciousness. Stars. Stars. I never see them in London but the night sky in Paris is full of them. I wonder how I will look in middle age when beauty and appeal and the sex drive, that impulse when a man is drawn to woman will fade. Life is poetry, my childhood in Dominica and women with their ammunition and their apparel. I never thought of other women as being in competition with me for the approval of men until the end of my first love affair. And then there was the poetry in my twenties. It cut me deep from skin to bone. I could feel it you know. There was nothing dysfunctional about the cut. Only I felt its power keenly, its voice, the chains and links of the voids therein. It stated wish fulfilment, commentary on modern issues and I felt it intensely at night when the world around me was asleep, when I felt drowsy or secretly despair at the situations and conflict I found myself in. Sometimes I even hated myself because I knew with some finality now that I had created the world I lived in now. There was no going back. Childhood, whatever state of mind, flux I had created then and now was over in a strong and futile sense. I could never get it back (whatever normal was). Normal was a word everyone used. It was a word everyone around me, even my family believed in. It was a word that depressed me. Was I a lady? I who was so ignorant of many things, that had so few belongings, not even a tiny flat or house with two bedrooms to my name, furniture that I could move and place in rooms as I pleased. Had I ever really been in love and loved? I believed that secrets should never be told. But I told my first husband everything. I wanted to believe that he loved me completely, that the past didn't matter. Back and forth I would go every night writing effortlessly in my black notebook. The past, history came with such ease. In this day and age the woman I had become was called a non-conformist. The norm was to get married before you were thirty and have children, a house, housekeeper, maids, a linen cupboard, have holidays, go camping, to the seaside. Of course I thought I would and could have all these things. I would have worked for it but shock and horror it did not come my way. I was left behind while others stronger than I was took that shot at the big time. I shook it, writing all my secrets down (the parts of me that just did not fit in this life, this city). I shook if off my chest like a fish hooked on a fisherman's line shook the breeze and seawater off its scales, and fins and back. Sometimes I thought to myself, 'Jean, you're missing out. You're missing out on life.' Sometimes I would say to myself, 'What if you'd just let yourself go a little? Talk a little, make a little conversation, be brave, braver, and confident like those mannequins in the window that you passed today with their chins up.' I thought I would only become illuminated as a woman when he, the man in my life stroked my cheek, my palm, my bottom lip, my head and it would always come with a rush of this feeling to my head. He is so pale and beautiful, so fragile and delicate, like a flower in the winter light. The hush of silence in the room is as soft as feathers. His breath is as fresh as water. His soul is perfect but he doesn't know this yet. I imagine it's a feeling he will only experience with his children and his future wife. Now he is a work in progress, caught between two worlds and enjoying the view. It is as pure as white-hot chemistry. His eyes are wet and dreamy. His hands and his fingertips are not delicate. They bruise the wasteland of my face easily. When I was away from him the world around me became cold. It felt like a feast of winter all around me. A heavy glow, inviting look, a picture of innocence colours your look of the world, of how to be loved. Tonight, I am an empress of cool in my dress and for a time now there has been no new money for new dresses. It hurts so much when he touches me on my arm, when he puts his arm around my shoulder I shudder. I can sometimes feel the chill wrapped in his embrace. His fingertips burn my skin, my lips. The only thing that soothes me is his kisses, his presence and the fact that now in the bedroom we are equal. Now submission, role-play, pain and pleasure are open to interpretation. He is gentle around me tonight, he is not angry, emotional or abusive, hurling abuse, screaming at me. His day must have gone reasonably well. This relationship doesn't heal anything in my past; bring emotional closure to the abuse I suffered in my childhood. It only serves to encase my newfound promiscuous behaviour in Technicolor in a bubble, in a grandiose time warp. I can't make him love me. Yet he is just as much impossible to love with his own mood swings as I am. I am always forgiving of his artistic temperament. I ask myself what is his heart, his soul trying to express. He's just as wounded as me. Comfort me, hold me just a while longer but he doesn't make eye contact with me, and speak to me. After making love I am as empty as a drum. I watch him sleep and feel fiercely protective over him. No love lost, only my innocence. Before I was invincible, and now in his arms I am fragile and delicate. From far away I hear myself say, 'Say something funny. Make me laugh.' He smiles, looks at me as if to say, 'I am not in love with you' but I don't care. For now, he is all mine. He belongs to me. His body, his jokes, the smell of his aftershave, his stories, his eyes, his lips so soft and delicate and bruising all at once. He is bitter. He is sweet. He does not believe in me, he does not believe me when I say that I love him. In my heart I say, I'll take you just the way you are, you maladjusted, maladroit, abusive, abused child from one abused, damaged and neglected child to another. He can see me and that is enough for me. I wash his back in circles, making ripples in the water with the palm of my hand, talking in circles but he doesn't say anything-meaningful back. I know he's just using me, humiliating me and causing a future exposure to trauma. I don't know any better, anything else, any other life. What is the reward, what is the payoff? Even when he humiliates me, he is still looking at me, working miracles on me. I have become an addict. It doesn't matter whether or not he speaks to me with contempt. I am convinced I have nothing without him. I am convinced I am nothing without him. Look at me, rescue me, save me; but the lost boys with vacant eyes and vague promises never do. They leave me feeling haunted and blue with ice water running through my veins. They never smile at you until you smile on the outside. If I am quiet it's because of the urgency in his voice, his breathing, his movements (himhimhim). Shame was a word I heard often when I was a weak child with a raving mother who often taunted me. And in this ice house there was no beauty, prettiness, loveliness, only grief, weariness, and a cry in the dark. I could not be alone and feel that kind of fire. And at that time in my life and in all the faces I saw around me all I saw and heard was, 'I do not, I do not, I do not love you.' And so order was spoiled and chaos ensued. I became frantic and believed that Lolita's passage had set my own. I kept my heart in a jar and my head in the sand. Everything happened so fast that I had no control over the pressure, the tightness of the close-knit and newly formed friendships, the disturbance, and the disturbances. I felt I could no longer live in a world that was not accepting of me. So I had to create a character in a storybook, a fairy tale to be loved, a glutton for punishment. For me he would bruise me to the bone, to my psyche. I'm a dazzling insomniac. Even my silent screaming when I am falling apart is dazzling with my every waking thought and living moment. I brought submission to the table. I had solitude on my side. He had a kind of self-leadership about him then. I was alive even in those empty moments. I learnt to say, if you feel like it then love me, if you don't then don't. I began to see his, my, our rituals as crucial turning points in the relationship. I could not bear being alone, being left alone. The headline read, 'Let's stop the persecution'. It could have been something I had written, perhaps a letter to the editor. I saw a flash, a slap against a face across the breakfast table and my sister gave a shout and began to cry. I remember washing my hair in a woman's salon and reading about the virgin lover in Nabokov's Lolita. My fingers holding onto the spine of the book, bookmarking the last page I read. The girl sitting next to me at the basin had doll eyes. They were brown with gold, golden flecks in them and so I began to learn what any woman would do for vanity in high school. As a child I grew up in a house made of brightness, made up of bright things. Tough love was a shiny bullet flying through the air. The surfaces were conservative, tense yet tidal, emotions running high, the collection of them and those experiences hard. And then I began to long for the weight of the meditative hush in leaves. It was the only thing that brought me peace of mind and that froze both joy and deception in their tracks. I wanted to be the sensible child taking the separation or divorce pretty well. I wanted to tell my mother that she hurt the people who loved her the most. But he, my father does not give of himself effortlessly or consistently. There were often closed doors. They would bang shut and it could be heard in all the rooms. It could even reach children who were supposed to be asleep, their ears. It couldn't have been that serious. I heard my mother laughing. She sounded free. Free in the sense that she was a young girl again without any limitations being placed on her. The limitations of a family and a husband and especially work. My mother and sister had the personality of a volcano. All I could taste was rain, pretend that I was dead in the sea whenever, wherever I heard a shriek of excitement on the beach from other children building castles. I imagined auras while their mothers dried their hair with a towel and gave them money, pressed silver coins in their hand for ice cream or for something cold to drink. Other children would parade and dance in front of their mother's. I wanted to be left alone. I was always a child on the verge of a nervous breakdown. As a young woman I wanted my gracious, appreciative heart to locate others. The art was not to fall like the virgin lover in Nabokov's Lolita. But fall I did. It was always cold where I was. It was not my dream to be endeavoured with literary pursuits from a young age. Children do not have the mental faculty to wish fear away in an instant. Children are just brave. They just seem to have that cosmic life force. I don't think I was a brave child. I wanted to be a volcano but I just didn't have that in me. And when I grew up into a young woman, into a writer, that oppressive feeling that I had to be emancipated in some or all the way never left me. It stayed with me at my side. It was my doppelganger. And as I became a vibrant type of person and my thoughts more and more vivid I could see all the beauty in the world around me except in me. All I could understand was people and write about them and me observing them. Playing dead in the water in the end had served me well and had taken me to new heights and had fostered an unseen intelligence. My father did everything but talk. Meanwhile I pulled out the entire minimum stops and shortcuts.

Purpose is life. The war inside my mind is often a war of nerves, a crowded house. It leaves me with a feeling of being locked up inside a box, Pandora's Box. There's place for stigma and being, the unbearable in there as well. Living in a fog-like consciousness, always watching the clock, that round island made up of numbers. So I had to discover that the universe promises the human condition two things: mortality and eternity. Depression doesn't come with a vision of the world. It comes with its own canvas, blank and its own personal mission, do or die, go beyond yonder. The proof of depression is something absurdly supernatural, that there is something greater than you are even if it is a calling and a gift in your blood. Your need to learn how to fly, the machinations of your consciousness 'caught by the river' by the river exploding into life in front of your eyes. Sometimes the story begins at the end or with flashbacks with dramatic effect moving forwards and backwards. It is blood that is thicker than water, than family bloodlines or the phoenix rising from ashes. Head against the brick and stone of depression is often a permanent protest. When I began to write poetry, I left space for interpretation, for kindred spirits and soul mates, even for ghosts. It is brutal, dissolves, deranges, distorts and it drums this in to you. It has such a presence, pain, depression, melancholia standing at attention. Poetry became my goal (the force of my reality, the reality I lived in) and my life. It became my desire that existed in both the spirit of place of darkness and light. It became the psychosomatic root to my cognitive thinking and my self-help. When you're depressed you keep your thoughts and reflections to yourself. They're more often than not charged with electricity, electricity that is not easy to shield yourself from like the eye of the sun. 'Come back to bed.' Your body says. Your eyes are vacant hinting at the spark and the glow of the displeasure of ill health, old wounds and escape. You feel naked, as if you've been abandoned in the dark, the pitch black and thrown to the wolves. I make lists of things that trouble me when I feel depressed. Any female writer would write what she feels destination anywhere in an upside-down world. Nothing fades away except the material world and the physical body. And so then I found myself in the city of cities, bereft, sinking my teeth into the polished floors of the library, the archives, the newspapers, textbooks, novels and biographies, anything that I could get my hands on and read. I was a film student marching across asphalt and green armed with books and not so often an engaging intellect. If only people were more like me, I wondered. If only people were not so mediocre. If only the other students did not spend their time drinking so much, not understanding me, sharing cigarettes. And then there was the woman with a feather in her hair, a modern-day witch. Her skin dark and ashy she would dance mad with rhythm in the halls of the ward in the hospital with feathers in her hair. I could not understand her, the mechanism, that shift within her brain, whatever was in her head, that swift shift in the chains of her consciousness like leaves against grass, Whitman's Leaves of Grass, Lewis Hyde's The Gift. It was here that I discovered Goethe. All I could think to myself was that this was madness and that madness could be as magnificent as the highs of euphoria. Nothing unique but as weeks went by it didn't seem to fade away into the comfort blanket world of inhibitory drugs and prescribed medication and that beautiful Lithium. I could only face the world with the psychology I gleaned from my reading, delving deep into the ghostly facets and facts of the unstable planet of illness and mental illness. I grew excited by the potential that lay ahead of me, in the distant future. It was always hours away. All I had to do was built on the edges of a dream. When I think of that time before my life began once more in search of a fabulous road, I seemed to live in a nation in ruins in that hospital, filled with ruined people, and lives that were intensely fragile. Their sadness

39

seeped into me like stains in the peeling wallpaper at the Salvation Army. I needed to feel alive and I could only feel alive when I was witnessing the pain of other souls and when I could tell and see how the world put pressure on them to excel. I began to live in books and on the plateaus and landscapes it offered me. I needed to picture a life without the cool order and routine of student nurses hovering, staring at a television's show. For now I needed that but I needed the world too. Dark, dark, dark and just like that it was gone. I am the way I am because of my mother, other women, my father, aunts and the hidden meaning in responsibility. I have felt devastation all my life, loss, people simply passing through my life going from one place to the next and I have found that words are the easy part. The outside world doesn't inform anything that you say or do when you are living with ghosts that you're waiting to be cured of. His eyes were a sea of green glass and his hair was long and dark. We could talk for hours sitting on the grass. I would stare into his eyes and that glass would chip away at the fragments of my heart. I even found time to fall in love and out of hate with my soul (what does it mean to have a soul) and with the being of myself. I found I could reconstruct the material, make it emotive, and make it glad. I wanted to bring my family back together again. I wanted to heal what was broken. All I saw around me were broken people, shattered people, people in recovery under daily observation and I was one of them. I felt as if there was some part of me that didn't belong to the world. Yonder, unbearable light, madness, illness, scar tissue, a heavy kind of woundedness can do that to you. And what are women truly at heart if the writers are the thinkers. Poets are dreamers and being conscious of their dreams they are conscious of the guts they have to live in this damned-if-they-do, damned-if-they-don't-world. We have to start somewhere I reckon, all women do. We are the ones who have to come up with a blank emotionally intuitive and spiritual

40

slate before our written words become imprinted on an audience, a reader, a woman, a man or a child. Before we burn away into nothingness, before we escape, and before truth stares us down in the face. Awareness and the grit in our souls always comes with nurturing and until there's an unbearable lightness in our awareness, a turn of the switch to develop this spirit in others. Our writing (female writing) only becomes more successful when we inspire others to gravitate towards greatness. From a youth's pure and angelic roots to being a walking mass of contradictions as they grow, to their bones, the consciousness of a movement has begun across the female nation reaching converging lines bordering on the universal. Writers' psyches cannot survive in dysfunction without the pictures of our external reality growing cold and dim as they fill inner space, marking turning points in time, in the flesh of history books. This is my message to the youth of the world. Pay attention to your dreams. The light in all of you is like a volcano. It can melt the heart of stone. Perhaps one of the loneliest experiences in the whole world is this, writing. I say this because on the surface I feel I can make it look effortless (there is a transference, a catalyst that I can't explain, can't put my finger on) while inside the vision we have this surface that if looks could kill it could kill. I've realised through my long walks that the woman who is secure in her home is the woman who has married, who has those children, who cooks those breakfasts and steaks, maintains a household, is the lady of the house. She is the madam who orders the kind of fish her husband likes to have. She puts honey and lemon in her tea, serves it like that when guests come to her house. Other women her age, other women with the same interests she has, who have the same number of children that she has. She does not have to put her coat on, her scarf, and her hat and open the door and walk out into the world a leper, yes, I say a leper because she is rejected wherever she goes. She is the Outsider, the loner, isolated. Nowhere is there a paradise for her. There are norms and values. What are the norms and values of a single woman (note I did not say the single 'lady')? A single woman is a burden to her family if she is unemployed. If she does not have any skills and her loveliness fades away swiftly. Nobody wants to have anything to do with her. They do not want to talk to her, converse with her because she does not have any talents. If she had they've already convinced themselves of this fact that she would've been married long ago, off their hands. She will never find herself in a field of love. Instead she will imagine what it would be like. She would imagine the atomic illusion of it. And she will know deep in her heart that she will be a girl for the rest of her life, a being who will never be swept off her feet by a masculine swagger. She would never understand what the words 'flirt', 'flirting' meant. She would remain detached from the world her cousins now inhabit, tangled in obsession. Men like to eat meat and she will remember meals she had with a man once or twice. How he licked the fat off his lips and drank his wine and how kind he was to her like her father was and when she thought of that she would always think of Dominica. You have to live. But I didn't know. I didn't know how to live, how to ask, 'Are you happy now?' All I seemed to say over and over again was, 'Are you happy now, Jean? Is this what you wanted, or was it a manifesto of loneliness and despair that I had been searching for all of my life since childhood?' All I knew was hotel room after hotel room, meetings there, situations there. I wanted to be filled bit by bit with love and empathy for other people who seemed to find themselves in the same situation I was in. They were lost. I was lost. I was scared to find out that I had no substance. I was baffled by the life around me and the lives people were living. It was as if they were telling me I was the fraud, the fake, and the poser. I still don't know how it came about, the writing part of me that bit.

Now when I come to my younger sister she is half otherworldly, half superimposed in reality. Now she is made of substance. God, why am I not. Why? So here I am? Why? I don't know what love is, what love is made of, why I am out of touch with that reality and I've been out of touch with it for a long time. So here I am in London where the lights aren't as bright as they are in Paris and in my dreams I was in Dominica. It was always playing at the back of my mind. There was nothing European about me although I had travelled on the continent. A man gave me advice once. I didn't take it. Oh, I pretend to listen and it's alright for them to know that I am just pretending too while they pretend to care about me. What are you thinking about in that intelligent little head of yours Jean? I don't think you need saving. I think you're fierce enough to understand your circumstances, to grapple with the future that lies ahead of you, to take it on. Not many women can do that. Are you lonely? Even I get lonely sometimes. Sometimes even when I'm surrounded by other people truly living. What does it mean to truly live? Does it mean to be happy, and content, the weight of a ravaged country or mountain off your back? Money does not make anyone happy. It can make you, give you a certain sense of power and control over other people but coming back to you, pet; you give me that impression that all 'little Jean' had known in a way her whole life was suffering. It is a reality I can't bear to face, to face this existence, this depression, this illness. You might think I'm brave but I don't think I'm brave. There is nothing heroic about miserable me I'm afraid. I sought out male companions who were pure of heart and failed miserably at that too. While leaves curled up (I too curled up in my bed at night), shrivelled up (my soul shrivelled up), winter danced away and seasons passed, turned into the loving of summertime I took to the streets again and little cafes. I casually observed the ballad of the human race around me and the wonder of

43

loneliness. It took guts to live and I was so meek, so week, mousy. I did not know how to live. Nobody had taught me anything about that. I had to steal it the best way I knew how. By using my brain as a catalyst and by filling black notebooks with the winters, the breath of the wilderness, the wild of life, the Technicolor of poppies in a field, drops of rain on a drab coat, shoes that looked a bit worse for wear. I wanted to remember Dominica (my choice). Not the suffering but the lavishness of the books I stuck my nose in the library when I was a child. It made me feel better. I too had a right to live in this world. You, anyone could not take that away from me. I was not a ghost although I moved like one through the streets. I have finally decided what my gift was to this world. Sacrifice. I am still here. Magnificently I am still all here. The unbearable light in having bright conversation, sharp, bright, intuitive eyes with insight into the world around sensitive me. I need a drink, badly, to forget all about yesterday. I'm pensive (don't give a damn about this maddening hell that seems to cavort beautifully, helplessly around me. I drown in its echo, its phenomena.) Am I cultured? Am I educated? I always wanted to be. I wanted to be a woman who is secure in her own home. I wanted to be a brutal thinker, a woman who has not been initiated into the sexual impulse (the wonder of a kiss, the virgin seed awakening to consciousness in a touch, love, beating heart, romantic interlude) at an early stage of her development. Poor me, hey. I don't think my mother ever knew how much she really hurt me. I think when I first became aware of that I became less trusting of the world around me. I became detached from it in a sense and there I was thrust into a state of imbalance. I could no longer feel the flux of equilibrium, fisherman's thievery, the glint of the silver skin of the fin of the fish. Love stories come from that place, the land of immortals. They truly last forever but love affairs are another equation, another seam, hemmed in by mirth, priorities and cons.

They're inelegant. A love affair drifts. You can't read its palm. It has a noose tied around its neck. It lost itself into the world like it has been there forever. It's just an obsession. It is just an obsession in an open love field. I met someone once. He smelled like the earth. His hands were rough. He wore a mask and I had one too but it didn't matter. It didn't matter that we couldn't define the boundaries of the relationship. He made me feel as if I could do anything, be anything, feel alive. It was as if I had just come into being, you know. And when it rained, I didn't feel the rain. When I was away from him the world no longer felt uninviting and cold, grave and condescending. I could look people in the eye because now I too was a possession. The dark no longer made a cripple out of me. It no longer burned me, that giant. I could close my eyes and fast forward to a time that I looked forward to. I no longer said, 'What is love anyway? It means nothing to me.' I would sit across from him at a table at a restaurant (he would order and he'd be in charge) and he would say things that would fill me with delight, with bliss, something would just shift inside of me. I would no longer be a girl; I would become a woman, a fashionable lady. I would sample everything on my plate. I would warm to him. The days when I felt persecuted by sitting idle while the world would go by would be long gone. He would colour my life now. He would lecture me not my subconscious, and not the inner spaces of my mind. I'd think to myself that now I have no more adversaries. Now I have my revenge. I only have to compete with other women who are in my position. My lonely days were over (not completely.) There was a part of me that knew that there would be a new area where desolation would await me. I would be hungry for more shades of energy, power, and love. As soon as the person or people in the next room or downstairs moved out, someone new would move in.

Aspects of Dickinson, the poet

If you are a poet, then you are family, then you are my family. You will forever be alive to me in the years to come, part of my history in life, and death. It is a sign of the times, my hot aching-masculine throat chanting, and chanting, and chanting into these early hours of the morning. There's distance between us. Madness. This is madness. This engagement, this relationship can never be. You're a man that I used to know when the bloom of youth was on my side. Now I'm old. Older. Less sure. You're a memory, or, rather a figment of my imagination, an illusion, an apparition like the half ghostlike-figure of Mrs Rochester gone mad in the attic, that nasty and miserable attic. I don't feel like writing today. It is cold outside. Humble leaf falls to the ground. Oh, even a leaf knows about the game of humility. After the winter, there's harvest. There's earth, and life, precious matter that survives the cold, the winter. I remember loneliness very well. Its slow torture. Its machinery like the wheels of a bicycle. Master, will you still think of me as bliss, as all of the above. You are, you will always be beautiful to me. Undecided, your mind filled with uncertainties (so, familiar to me, but unfamiliar to you), you left. In other words, father sent you packing, so, no romance for me, no courting, or engagement. You left me. The friendship now totally, totally forgotten, but the poet in me speaks, the woman in me listens, the class system I belong to tolerates, and my heart, and mind understands completely. You had to wound me, to save yourself. I know I am intense. I have a hectic personality that no man will ever find attractive. This I know. This I have some knowledge of. I am shy when I meet new people. I don't go out much. I don't go to gatherings. I was an excellent student at the seminary, but that was a world that too soon came to an end. I had to move on, live my life. Understand this. I chose this life; this life did not choose me. I have mastered the artistic life. The periods of mental wellness I find invigorating. The periods of creativity, they come, and they go, and they bring me much torment, feverish distress that can only be broken by the company that I keep. Imagination is a spell, or rather, spells. Tea leaves at the bottom of a porcelain teacup, but no fortune-teller am I. I am just a daughter who has that most rare of commodities, a rebellious nature, a perfectionistic-streak within her. Master, tell me all the ways that I have to love you. Your face is cherished. It is the one face I want to see for the rest of my Amherst days. Be my friend, or, nothing at all, because friendship is all that I can offer you. One day, perhaps they will say that the only males in her life were men old enough to be her father. She gravitates to them, they in turn gravitated towards her, her virginal-innocence, her thoughts, youth, the bloom of youth, and I suppose that, yes, there was an absence of that in their lives. You see, they were middle-aged, reaching that crisis of faith in their lives that all mean reach in middle age. They will, the critics, the public, will say that she loved them, in return they gave her the world that her childlike-possessive mother had not given her. Sadness, vast disagreement, an intense, yet natural reaction to difficulty, a brief history of melancholy, dark fluid inside my body. My diet governs my body, clinical depression, brain chemistry, balance of chemicals our response, discerning the value of sadness, inevitable, you've missed out, in gaining wisdom, increase wisdom increase sadness, profound joy, here comes the cycle of life, needs, evolutionary level, stages of bonds, familiar and comfortable, balance, temperament, sadness measuring grief probing its structures, gathering pain like a net of fishes, feathers, heartbreak bird in the bush, bird in the universality of my hand, emotional pain, don't suffer. You don't have to suffer, her eyes seem to say, articulate, express, hope. Let me write a poem about hope. Shades of bloom govern, structures building a muscle, the muscle of the poetry. What happened, what happened to you. Pay attention to me, give me your approval, your sincerity. I am feeling lost, withdrawn from the world, an average life, who wants an average life, only the followers, only the disciples, not the saints, question of pain, existential identity, what can I do, stuck, rat in the wheel, bird in a cage, other goals, plans, results, take responsibility move repetitively, logically, hymn, with force I take you, sounds, sounds, sounds, quiver, tomb, winds, rain, weather forecast, Outcast, caravans of it, knit, company close afterlife immortality flood, composed death in sensuous ironic stages untouched roof of scooped surrender snow field harvest, mid-19th century, way of life, her room looked out at the cemetery like me, tomorrow I might be gone, or survive to live another day, to see paradise, she/I writes about death, the perspective of the majority of death, the scarcity of life, the minority of love, minor is loneliness major is the brethren at the Assembly of God, major is the earth. So, I have this room. I wake up in the morning and the first thing the room (yes, the room speaks to me with a voice as loud as thunder), the first thing the room says to me is, "So, when are you going to start afresh, write something new." Or it is just a voice that says, "Write! The world is waiting upon you. It is necessary for you to write." The verses are always wholesome. I don't have to negotiate too much between reason, and doubt, being outclassed by other young women of this era, financial security (we are quite well-off, father is prosperous, my brother will soon follow in his footsteps), and the insecurity the work of writing brings with it. I don't feel the need to go out into society, be the most beautiful, or sophisticated young woman in the room, asked to dance, or walk outside, and take in fresh air with a male companion. Why bother? The family, father, says I pretend not to care. That I'm too rebellious for words. That I should accept the Christ as my living Saviour. As soon as I accept Jesus Christ, father says my loneliness will disappear as if it never existed. But I know through trial and error that although I despise the loneliness sometimes, I must live with it, submit to it, obey its calling. It is service, under my jurisdiction. I already have the world, you see. In my frame, in my psychological makeup, in the capacity of my physical body, my intellect never wanes. I think of the wildflowers out in the fields of Amherst. From them there is no escape. Do I long for an exit, the way I long for my father, and brother's approval, sometimes, sometimes. In the hush of the moonlight when I am writing, I am utterly alone, the house is asleep, but I don't feel timid, or feebleminded when I write. I'm beautifully composed. The words come to me as a flood. Their clarity of vision, movement, and moods are distinct, and I am calm, utterly, utterly calm, charmed too by the rhythm of writing. The voice, and the vision of the writing. Oh, how I do love that word, 'vision'. Its wakefulness, and process of reckoning, it's a sacrifice to be a woman on your own, its progress, the pace of its world that comes in vibrations of sea waves, in oceanic patterns. No Ophelia am I. I am as calm as the storm whenever I write. Sometimes I think I am a woman, but when I write I become a man, mannish, because in these days it is only acceptable for a man to write. I am the volcano lover versus that storm. One day I will be gone forever, then father says to me, asks me plaintively, "Emily, my daughter that I love so, so, much, my dearly beloved that is the apple of my beguiling eye, will you go to heaven, or will you go to hell. Hell is damnation. Your soul will be damned." I say nothing when they all start behaving like this, or, I go to my bedroom. Sit, wait, and the 'flood' comes. I thought, once, there would come a day when I would captivate a man, set his world, his soul, his spirit on fire. That we would become engaged for a year, or perhaps longer than that, give or take a few years, but I've had to move on, with difficulty, with a kind of tenacity that I never knew I had within me, I clung to life sometimes, frightened of the low depths I sometimes go to, that abyss, that territory, that darkness. I know I have shamed our family in this close-knit community by not going to church with my family, but I think that God understands what matters to me after all. Art, art, art, I come undone under the touch of your nimble fingers, your beautiful hands, your sensitive, and engaging face. All art s life lit up for the entire world to see on public display. I have such an undying affection for the 'flood'. It is like the garden to me. It is precious seed. And I am, of course I am, the seed thief. A seed thief who lives in both reality, and non-reality. On display, on exhibition, subject to judgemental indifference, and moods, and disapproval. As a child I looked up to father, but now we have words. He cross-questions me about the church, don't I want to have a relationship with the son of David. I tell him, that in no uncertain terms do I want to be indoctrinated by rhetoric. And who created man, did God create man, or did man create God in his image. I can't stand those stories of temptation in the garden. I think to myself, 'poor snake, poor serpent with the forked tongue, maybe you got the raw deal, instead of Adam, and the Eve created from his rib'. Sometimes I think aloud. I shouldn't misbehave, or throw tantrums, or fits, but I do when I reach the end of my tether. I have to write. It keeps me sane, and awakened to the intrinsic environment around me. I internalise, internalise, internalise. What else can I do? It keeps the 'flood's' vein sated, and alive. There is a golden reconciliation there between the education of the mind, and the psychology of the brain. What is intelligence anyway, does it make father, or my brother happier entities? They look the same to me. Stressed by the burdens, and cares, and triumphs of the day, in much the same way as I am. Then, suddenly one afternoon, after resting, after working in the garden, (which is a labour of love to me). Unabashed I spoke my mind, my dazzling mind that I find so hard to free sometimes, to let go of, talked in the room as if there was another person in the room with me, covered up my lips, breath is warm and sweet, major is church, tireless community worker like my father, secure intrusion, moments' of value, worthwhile appreciation, demands intense, letter after letter, they couldn't do it, stylistic brilliance, worm country is a vain country, subjects art is a motel, messy, angst, growing older, friendship failed, she asked too much, like me, parallel, question, solution translated into deity, the saved, I ask too much. I want it all. I need everything. I desire love, not the lack of it. Society does not belong to me, unmoved, choose one, or don't choose at all, there were moments, anguish, withdrawal of love, speaking about being a poet, will to breath where you are, sorrow, suffering is nearby, thinking of you, yours forever, male muses, triumphant, paradise, is heaven, nothing does justice to your voice, your face, holding onto the past can kill you, futile, done with, the compass navigating me relentlessly like the spoke of a wheel, the normal non-existence, talk difficulty, exhausting, she exhausts you, encounter, great trees and a garden, flame of a girl, flame of a woman, bright, childlike. I will always be childlike, for that is what the life is like for a spinster, Mr Fatman also discouraged my poetry, fame, celebrity, world, world famous, spasmodic, uncontrollable, no master in my life, organize to bare my soul, have it out if you will with rebellion and, interior power lies risk, taboo, unnatural to be alone, it would be real life to love you, to long for you, to belong to you, the gaze, the gaze, the gaze, your face full of grace, your shoes caked with mud, sun slinging warmth, the heat of the day, give me the light of the day over and above despair. Creativity in crisis, in hallucination, distress, distraction, separated, detached, feeling powerless, no self-possession. salute me, freezing, salute me joyful, or don't salute me at all, the hours, the hours touch equality, liberty, noon is paradise, euphoria, drama of the short story, one pities her, one pities me, much more urgent, saying something, requires urgent attention, the nerves Egyptian like Cleopatra, a wooden, stale piece of bread recollected, stupor, do you know of it, want of it, master. kidneys, Emily Dickinson, mental state, Elizabeth bishop, Plath, early Sexton, early poems, girlish, those general attractive, penetrating, 70 years after her death, altered, 2000 poems. So, I add titles, punctuation, authentic and sincere was her offering to the world, voice of Eve, Eve's seed, thirst, common sense, found in that voice, what it feels like to be alive, march to progress, marked by process, circumference, equilibrium, greater than the loss of my master, is the craft, is the imagination, crowned, erect, equal, living, the props, the posture of the house. I withdraw into my bedroom, my desk, just like her, just like her, see, see my soul, look at my hurting, my suffering, my shame is hard too, lot worse background, you were saved, restored, reconcile, personal views taught, learned. We built Amherst. This is our town, my town. You're brave, and bold, and a brilliant thinker, Master. There's a funeral inside my head. Solitude is important to me. The soul, the poet, Abigail George, in her bedroom. Both women, set in their ways, and habits, set categories for their poems. One, with the bright flame of her lamp light, the other with Edison's lightbulb. Alone in her bedroom daylight turns into hours, into afternoons. Emily Dickinson, not the poetess Emily Dickinson to be sure, is finding herself gardening, doing household chores, this genius by lamplight, who first defined farewell to a dark idea, and then the sea of farewell to visions and voices. Rivers hurry pass me by. Remote me marked with hope, sweetness, madness near, it either gives or takes. The skill of language, she was free, never scolded, restless, do justice to the poem, I tell myself, do a kindness on impulse, let that be the stimulus for the natural environment, the supernatural, anonymously, the mystery of the poet, Amherst, Massachusetts.

Books, I am surrounded by a paradise that is all mine. Kept an eye, nobody ever said that the writing fit their reality, fugitive little waves making sparks of electricity, forgotten about when they vanish into thin air, waves- patterns of waves. There are more Christian sisters, more brethren, more non-supportive sons, more girls, more boys vastly mysterious to me, greater than fugitive. They laugh at me like, and the wilderness hums, suggestion, real life, real life, what is that, no control, powerful, optimistic, Kafka, Kant, riding peak, exploring wave, dynamic of the sea, the potential of sense, common sense numb, creep across my psyche, solitary, break through broke, plunged into abyss, the seed project, outside of that frame, that tradition, advanced, education, healthy psychological, emotional, husband father define who they are, as women, image of the girl, submission, Sir Thomas Brown, Mrs Browning, metaphysical not confessional, carpenter, bird, being, feeling and metaphor, feeling and metaphor, abstract, is conditioned-thinking, anoint, anoint, anoint, impatient, goal female missionaries like my mother wanted me to become, to marry an Irish missionary, walking to find flowers, wildflowers, I walk with angels, I talk to angels, the angels sing, I listen, nature was apart from her, nomadic here, there, science, religious lecture, botanist, she knew the stars, space gaps her peers had fellow pupils, love, love Jesus, doubt him, skepticism, only on faith, sound stands ghost-like, philosophy, guess contempt, crucifixion, redemptive, plucked in this vein, the soul, the soul, the soul, the art student, standing alone a rebel linger at doorways, pause with my lamp, it is hard for me to give life to Amherst, outcast like me, orthodox-belief, tragic Christianity, like me daughter didn't go to church, the poetic life, name dropped like childhood, porcelain teacup, fall from grace into struggle, my rank now spinster, half-unconscious, erect, reject, isolate by will, by inter-faith, rhythm, shadowy figure, invalid, bewildering, I never had a mother, what is a burden, never intimate, she became like a child in my arms.

Anonymous, the virgin slate

The argument was about nothing really. I really cannot remember who started it first. It was between a girl, barely out of adolescence and her married boyfriend. Perhaps I told him that I did not think that my mother really loved or accepted the choices I made in my life and that I thought he could be supportive of me. Was he really listening? Girls need their mothers more than they need their fathers. Girls need devoted parents. All I could feel was emotional. He was cold and non-committal. I knew my place and he knew his. I wanted to scream at the top of my lungs was, 'Listen to me, please!' I already knew it would be ignored.

'We're not making love anymore?'

'So what? We can do other things. We are not in the primitive ages anymore. We can talk. You know what I want. I want a married life.'

'That's why I have a wife. I can talk to her.'

'This is not a relationship?'

'I know this is not a relationship.'

'All this talk is making me depressed.'

'Go home. Go home to your family, lady. Go home to your mother and your father.'

'Why do you want to hurt me?'

'This is the end of whatever dream you had.'

'Of, course, I can see that. I can see it when you look at me. Please don't talk to me like this?'

'You want me to tell you that I need you. I don't need you. You don't need me as much as you think you do.'

'I'm in pain. Can't you see that?'

'Yes, you're in pain. You are giving me a headache. Go away. Leave me alone and stop calling me. What if my wife picked up? What then?

This is not love. When people treat each other this way. This, this is not love.'

'When you were young did you ever map your life out? Of who you were going to get married to? Your wife? Your life? Your children?'

'You'll grow up and then one day you'll wake up and I'll be the last thing you remember. The last thing on your mind. You will not have to put me on your itinerary. You won't have to make as if you cook and clean on my account.'

'We always fight. I realise that now.'

'Good. Then leave.'

'Please?'

'Go. Just go. In the end you'll see it is better that way.'

'Talk to me. Humour me. Tell me a story about a lost, frightened girl who comes to the big city with a myriad of dreams. In the end, none of her dreams comes true. She sleeps with men in hotels. She is hurt. Flesh is flesh. What happens to a lady and a man? Do they meet and always fall in love? What happens then is that nothing good comes from it? The man leaves and she does not have any self-worth.'

'You don't deserve this. The way I have treated you. Go out into the world. Make something of yourself. You are young. You are attractive. That is the dream world, the high art of the female outsider. I need to know that you are going to be fine about this.'

'You need to know that you are fine with the fact that you are ending my world as I know it.'

'Do you want to smoke?'

'I don't smoke. You know that.'

'You need to relax. So, this is the first time then for you.'

'Men have left me before. This is not the first time. You were not the first. You are going to make me cry. Maybe it is best if you don't say anything anymore.'

'Have a cigarette with me anyway.'

'Cigarettes make me cough. They taste terrible.'

'You never complained before. Now you are complaining.'

'Things were different before. By that, I mean I was going to see you again. I was happy that I was going to see you again. I would have done anything in the world for you, you know. I know how to love someone. Someone even like you. Someone powerful and insecure and full doubts and insecurities.'

'So, you have discovered a man's secret at last. That we are much more vulnerable than a woman.'

'And no doubt I will keep discovering it over and over again. I really do not mind if you smoke that last cigarette now. Let me just find my shoes and the rest of my clothes. I'll go now.'

The world is not my home. Everything in this world seems to be a test or temporary. Fading out as the sunset at the end of the day or illuminating human flaws, truths that are eternal for us. We are indulgent creatures. We need trust. We need loyalty. We need kindness. We need family even though children can be selfish brats sometimes and husbands and wives and friends. We flirt. We flit. We make nests and then when they are empty there is a depression that never leaves us and that is why children come home for the holidays. The unseen is eternal. Ghost stories. Christmas. Fish. I have left childhood behind. They were gifts of great spiritual maturity. The psychiatrist teaches me how to let go, surrender if you will but how does a person let go of the only world (childhood) that she (I) have ever known. All is gold. We speak about the feelings of being emotionally bankrupt. Unable to deal with the voices in unison in society that are blocking mine out. She

57

says I also have to be heard. People have to listen to me too. Gone are the passages of contentment in books. I have no time to waste on something that I feel does not exist for me or for those who live in spiritual poverty. I have to learn how to love, how to marry but my parents were not good examples of this. I have to own this space, she says. I am a dreamer. I am a dreamer who has goals, as I am sure Virginia Woolf had goals with the relationships she had, with her writing, with her diaries and letters, with her marriage. Perhaps I desire the same things she did. In her lifetime. In her world. Who made up the rules anyway? I had a bad past and then I think of Alice in her terrifying trippy wonderland. Woolf knew of gender betrayal, constructing sympathy for her characters in her novels. Her hair as fine as Whitman's blades of grass. Woolf's words come in waves. They cut me deep. Their serious depth, desolate isolation, rejection and suicidal despair is there for the world to see, to read. As an adolescent, Woolf was already an intellectual. As an adolescent, I was already an intellectual. There was no psychoanalyst for her violent madness. Her outbursts. Sometimes I think I cannot walk down that road again. It is not a sunny road. It is not the road to Oz. There is a landmark exhilaration when dawn comes as if to say light beckons now, awake! With the light comes the awareness of a new day, vitality and energy for the nerves in your brain cells. Night comes with the same minutia. It is only now that the sun has faded away. The moon and the tapestry of stars is out. Lovers embrace in dark bedrooms across the world but I am in mourning because I cannot be with that one man who changed my world, who changed my world with one caress. A precarious touch and instantly there is a change in my suffering and my head, my biology was wired differently. The lonely cannot exist. Spiritually they die. The identity is decaying as they speak, walk, and think, constructing sentences, a string of verbal and non-verbal communication. So, what if I am a virgin again. Virgins thinks of sensuality and sexuality just as much as other people do but differently. Sensuality becomes noble. Sexuality becomes an electric waiting game. Why are there all these games in this life, in this world? Sexuality is not something that is alien to the virgin. She reads about it. Sometimes when she reads about it, she will think of her infertility, her breasts, her shoulders, the nape of her neck. The physical parts of her body that are the most sensitive to touch. Sometimes when she reads about it, she will blush. The weather is comic. First, there is sun, and then it is as if rain clouds are gathering and then the sun comes out again. I think of the dark room. I think of the lovers and how I will never be a part of that world again. It hurts too much to think, to breathe over what I have lost. What is a man? What is an older man? Grey hair at his temples. Wisdom beyond his years. Influence within his reach. Power. Powerful. Kings of their empires. Trophy wives at their sides or their best friends. Children. Children. Children. The children I will never have. What is love? Instead, I have research, my writing, and those are things that I am passionate about. I am a feminist but I am also a daughter who is still a child. Wanting attention. Wanting approval. Wanting gifts. I need a change of suffering. World did you hear me? I need a change of suffering. It is time women begin to listen to each other. It is time we all called each other feminists. It is a new word for me. Feminist. What does it mean? It has its own beauty. It has its own identity. The tragedy of the relationship that faltered is that it was both romantic and playful as it neared its end. The mood was spiritual and pensive. He was the land and I was the sea. My hands and feet were made of clay. Easily melted away by water. While his empires were made of (guess), steel girders planted into the ground, held down by gravity. He destroyed me. With every measure of success, that he acquires he lives on now in relative wealth. I live with my parents. From here on out it, life is an unknown destination. From here on out life is unpredictable. I am 35 going on 40. Silence is wonderful when all you hear is birdsong. Backyards have their own wisdom. Trees seem to fill that precious hour. Pour into your humanity. This, this is my tribe. Nature. Time is precious. So is life. They are sacred. I am an arrangement of combinations of particles, matter, opportunities, challenges, threads, cells and platelets that communicate with each other. Just as Virginia Woolf lined her pockets with stones and stepped into the River Ouse. Just as she communicates to me from the world or the region that she is in now, the beautiful drowning visitor I communicate with the profound and the concrete. The lake's surface is built like concrete. Perfect for skating but the skin, the fabric of what she was wearing, her shiny forehead is down there somewhere. Winter in the end. It is always winter in the end that rises up to meet me. In my dreams, there is a remote area in Greenland. Like the end of winter, we do not always remember childhood. It gives itself to us in dreams after the innocence; the light goes out in the world of a child. How we appear in our parents' eyes, in the end does it matter? It only really matters if we are happy individuals who become happy adults instead of functioning in dysfunctional households. Women keep on meeting different men all the time, up close and personal. Women want intimacy. Men want sex. I loved that book. Instead, I gave it to him. A boy. A man. I cannot remember which posture his shoulders and his height was brought to my attention. Thinking that it would heal some part of me. The broken parts of me. Parts I had misplaced so deep that I hoped nobody could find them. I needed music and he was my source of everything. Romanticism, pleasure, pain, intimacies and finding desolate landscape after desolate landscape but the truths that I found in the book was not the same for him as it was for me so I had to give up on him. He could not be my Leonard Woolf. It took me a long time to work him out of my system. 'Have you ever seen a man naked? You don't have any reason to be afraid. I am not going to hurt you.' He makes a ceremony out of everything. Lighting the candles, pouring the wine and giving me a glass of wine that I pretend to drink in tiny sips. Incense and scented candles are burning. I can even smell the scent of roses. Does every female writer ever have an experience of lesbian passion? Echoes in a wasteland. Images from a wilderness. The female writer is an intuitive. She is a catalyst. I lay on the bed in sweltering Durban thinking, if only he knew. Would it matter? Would it make a difference? I knew why he wanted to see me. It was not for conversation. He meant to educate me. I had come such a long way. From Johannesburg to Durban for this. For this charade to play itself out. That I was innocent. That I was so delicate my bones could break. I would be staying a week in his flat. I knew we would not leave to see the sights. Durban had beaches and restaurants that served up spicy Indian cuisine. Of course, he was going to hurt me. Of course, he was going to break my heart but there had been a line filled with monsters, beasts, and men, wolves, older men before him who had pressured me into doing something I did not want to do. Who had in the end made it out to be my idea? Then there was one man who wanted to photograph me, another who wanted to call me by another name. Probably the name of a lover who had left him or the other way around. I feel his mouth against mine, that slight pressure. His breath is warm. His mouth, his lips are dry. What was his name again? He did something important. He was on television. He made a lot of money. He was engaged. He had a son. So young. Youth wasted. I have always wanted the qualities of a young mother.

'Take your clothes off but do it slowly.' He said authoritatively.

'Why?' I asked shyly.

'You haven't done this before so I want it to be special for you. I want you to feel safe, comfortable. Aren't you happy with me? With everything that I've done for you today?' he whined. Yes, I could hear a whine in his voice. He was so close. We were too far into this game and so I had to go ahead with it. I had to go ahead with this snowball effect. He had paid for everything. Paid me to come here. Met me at the bus. Carried my suitcases.

We ate leftovers. Cold pizza. Yes, he had paid for this sexual transaction well in advance. I thought to myself. What was I supposed to say to that? He did take me to the beach. I was not hungry. I did not want anything to eat. I could see he was crestfallen by this. I knew instinctively that I had to make it up to him somehow but how, but why? I felt foolish for coming. He thought he knew my reasons for coming. That I was in love with him. He was the fool and not me. I could have laughed aloud but he had gone to all this trouble of making me feel safe and comfortable. Now I am home, 35, and over a decade later. What brings me bliss is cooking? It is therapeutic. Life is made up of moments. Some happy. Some unpleasant that sound like Verdi, Chopin and Tchaikovsky. There is something special about behaving as if it is the end of the virgin's world. You become a woman. What does that mean exactly? I am seeing a new psychiatrist after my last nervous breakdown. The new pills seem to be helping me cope. It is funny how a psychiatric patient does not need or want sex. You seem to lose that impulse, and that sex drive. Where does it go? What happens to it? Is it numbed? There is shark-infested waters out there. There is evil and danger. They are called men. The thirst for relationships has left me. Once again, I am an empty vessel.

'Mum, how are you?' I felt the coins in my jean jacket. I wanted home. I wanted mum.

'Fine. Why are you calling? Is something wrong?' I could hear the whine in her voice.

'No. Nothing.' I replied. I hummed.

'Your friend. Your girlfriend. Is she nice? Where are the both of you staying? Are you getting a lot of sun?' She seemed to perk up a bit.

'Everything is fine.' Why was I lying? Why did I run away from home again? Was it because of the complex and complicated relationship I had with my sad, elegant, longsuffering mother? Why did I do this to her? My father had left us. He was there physically but he had left us to our own devices. Two women on their own. A single parent had to be both mother and father. I could blame the anorexia on him. The distant father who wanted a social life and a wife who could be an active participant in that world. He wanted someone who would attend functions on his arm, smiling and nodding her head, looking out for him. Two women on their own. My mother did not really understand mental illness. Then one day unexpectedly he returned. After a hospital stay. We were father and daughter, hostile tributes aside that had to count for something. With my mother away in Johannesburg, my father and I confide in each other now. Frank talk exposing illness. Everything else was forgotten. I look at my books. No one will ever know where it really came from. No one will know the man who really inspired me to the wuthering heights, who helped my gift along. One day as I have said before I will never have youth on my side. Youth is wasted on the young. Will this make me bitter or crazy down the line? I am already crazy. I am already too thin. The skin and bone of an anorexic woman has many ghost stories to tell. Skinny legs. The flesh of a bird. I feel it in my bones. I feel the lonely life of crazy in my bones. It was planted there somehow like a sonnet, keys to a post-apartheid future. Psychoanalysis is filled with statements. Wrecks with gut symmetries. Frail beauty. Here humanity becomes relentless as they once did at the discovery of treasure after treasure in the wilderness of the rural countryside in another life. Writers are dreamers. Dreamers who plunge into all the universal symbolism has to offer. Expressions of suffering, heritage and knowledge. Is writing a book like childbirth, a Darwinian experience, a sensorial experiment, an engagement? The problems with symbolism are that it gives us a sense of our own mortality. A sense of false hope. In a dream, we might come upon a cauldron of water. What does this mean? The only thing that fits that kind of dream-reality in our existence is the warm sea, destination anywhere of the shoreline, the swimming pool or to go bathing in a river, wading into that weight of water. Once upon a time, we too were fish. Once upon a time, we too were intuitive children. Mushrooms are beautiful delicate things. The melons for this time of year are beautiful too. Food is too glorious for words. Food is like sex. We need it for our survival. If we do not have children to follow in our footsteps who will write history over repeatedly. Light comes in waves. They come in their own time. Their own medium of survival therapy. Their own ceremony in the shadows. The real world, reality, sanity, normal is a trap. Light is made up of the angelic. It is made up of the otherworldliness against the common particles of this world. I have gone so high. I have crashed romantically trying to live with the decisions I have made. Atonement can be beautiful like videotape. There is no room for lies only a lighthouse, only fulfilment, only videotape. A man can have sexual fulfilment. For a woman fulfilment is mingled in her blood, if she can see her unborn children in her lover's eyes. Had Virginia Woolf known love? Real love with Vita Sackville-West? What did she think of marriage? I write for women and I write for men. I am a feminist and a humanist but the question is can I be both. I have also known lesbian passion but it was never quite enough. It was driftwood. It was cats and dogs. It was a constellation. It was the red shred of a balloon in the hand of a screaming child. It was paste. It was a vital breathing lesson. It was gold and bright and illumined my world for a fraction. It was the investigation of a distillate. I feel a disembodiment when I talk about that time, feeling her fingers in mine, brushing her hair out of her face. I feel that there are apparitions inside my head. They come with their own prepared speeches, airs and graces. These damned adventurers. Did Virginia Woolf write enough, too much, or too little? Would she have liked to have children, a child, and a son? What is so dead wrong with married life for me? Would I not grow if I had companionship, if I had love, if I had someone to take care of me? Someone to lean on. Sometimes I feel so cold. My nerves tingling in my hands as if in this universe there are other worlds out there that are magical, stranger than fiction, haiku, Mr Muirhead, famous people. Now I am older but am I wiser? Ghosts. Ghosts. Ghosts. They all have their own stories to tell. What the hell? I kissed a girl, have slept with men. Have known love as Woolf's Orlando in my dreams and reality. There is this other feeling. I cling to things. To beautiful things. It is the feeling you get inside your heart as you find the words inside your head when you sing along to your favourite song on the radio. Who was she? Who was Virginia Woolf? Will the real Virginia Woolf please stand up? Will everyone who is anyone please stand up and give Virginia Woolf a standing ovation for making it so far, thus far? Was her life complete or incomplete? The sea. Trough. Crest. Trough. Crest. The waves emit their own frequency. I have the season ticket for the swimming pool. There are two hardboiled eggs for everyone for breakfast. Toast galore. A wasteland of breakfasts in middle class homes. The accomplished man that I see in front of me does not care for me anymore in any way. I am the least of his worries. Now I must survive. My mother is no longer at the height of her awareness as a bride. She no longer has those virginal mental faculties within reach, that ego of an adolescent girl now that she has brought children into the world. I must swim. I must regain something that I have lost. I must recover. I must evolve for a revolution from within to take place.

Bessie Head, her alter ego

I am tired. I look at other women in the ward and I see that they are tired too. It is hot. There is nothing that I can do to escape this intolerable heat. I lie under this sheet in this hospital. The doctor said I should just rest. Close my eyes and try and get some rest. There is nothing else they can do for me. But I have come to this nothing-place in this nothing-district to get away from my past. This too shall pass. The woman next to me keeps looking at me strangely. Are you God? She asks me. Some days it is, 'Do you know his son Jesus Christ?' She has a bible. She refuses to eat. Nobody visits her. Nobody visits me but that is because nobody knows where I am. There are ancient lives under Botswana's sky. I found when I used to be a journalist in another lifetime when I wrote about people in that distant past there used to be something urgent about it but something unfinished as well. Writing also saved my life, having a child and a man in my life. But the doctors, the nuns here say I will go out of my head if I think that way. They say that everything is for the best now. I can go and sit outside today. It's a beautiful day. Warm and sunny. Every day there was fruit at the hospital. Yesterday we had mangoes. The mango's flesh tasted wonderful. It reminded me of my childhood, of my sister, the warmth of a pinch of cumin offered to a supper meal, a country to call my own and the girl I was once. Not like some of those coquettish ones but a unique who suffered from anticipatory nostalgia from one moveable feast that she found from one book to the next. A woman received some avocados in the ward and she shared it amongst her friends. I spooned the ripe olive-looking flesh out of the skin and sucked the threads off my fingers. Beautiful. I asked my doctor for some pages or a notebook and a pen that I could write with. I felt I had something to say when he asked what it was for. Sometimes the heat here in

Botswana smells like incense burning. It goes to my head and stays there for ever after. Lovely. Poignant. Fresh. Burning sweetly reminding me of my female intuition. This heat has saved me. It has slowed all the racing thoughts within my head and they're all within my grasp now.

'Tell me Bessie do you have any friends here at the hospital. People who you can talk to.'

'Friends? Tell me what the meaning of that word is doctor. To stay here does not mean it is a permanent residence. I will move on from here as I have done before. It is not good to remain tied down, make bonds with people, and form relationships that will probably only hurt you in the end. I have found that out the hard way. Breaking ties with people, oh, I've done that my whole life.'

And for a long time, the doctor and I sat next to each other saying very little. We spoke about the weather and poetry and bananas of all things. Yes, of all things in the world we spoke about bananas. Bananas dominated the conversation when we eventually came around to speaking about it.

'Doctor, are you happy? Are you happy with your life? If you could go back to the past what would you change?' I ask plaintively.

The doctor looked out into the distance. There was a lovely breeze

'Lovely breeze Bessie, don't you think? You're very serious this afternoon. What has got you to think so deeply? Are you feeling morose?'

'Perhaps I am. But there have been times when thinking morose has saved my life. I've either stored enough of it away or not enough. And when it comes to those times of not feeling good enough, I take to my bed, pull the sheets over my head. I don't need friends.

Everybody needs a friend but I don't believe that people need friends in life. So, are you, happy, doctor?'

'Don't I look happy, Bessie?'

'I don't know. Are you?'

'Today this morning a nurse misplaced a file. I was not happy about that. But I had a hot cup of tea, a slice of cake, and a sandwich. Soon I will return your notebook. Perhaps you should think of going for a walk with the other patients.'

The notebook has saved my life but I don't tell the doctor that.

'Wake up. Wake up all you blasphemous fools. All you fools that are sinners. All you Judases that have betrayed God with a kiss. Blasphemy. Blasphemy. I now pronounce you man and wife. You may kiss the bride. Speak now or forever hold your peace. Jesus wants you for a sunbeam. Michael row your boat to shore. Repent, you wicked sinner or you will never receive salvation.'

I pretend I am fast asleep. I can hear her walking up and down in the room. She is wearing sandals. Soft like ballet slippers. Another woman is sobbing into her pillow at the far end of the room. 'Make her stop doing that.' I hear her say but nobody comes to make her stop.

'Are you awake yet? Wake up. I have good news for you. It is the coming of the Lord, the father of our Jesus Christ, son of David.'

'Wake up.'

And every time she walks past my bed, she says those words. And finally, I turn my head and play dumb, nodding my head. In a way it is soothing to know that the religious part of me that was always there within, along with my faith, my values, and my spirituality has never ever left me. It is only the woman in the bed next to me. The aliens have contacted her and they have a message for our government or she can see into the future and the human race have to be saved or she is a modern female version of Nostradamus. It has saved my life. This needful thing of people needing friends. God, I love you Botswana.

All my life I have carried this yolk of being an only child, the shroud of being an orphan has shadowed me all my life. I wonder now what it would be like to have grown up in a family with other sisters and brothers and to find rainbows everywhere you looked even in the Sudan, in the desert, in Kenya, in Ghana. When it comes to the wife and kindness you will find her in rooms. But I did not find my mother there. My mother was White. My father was Black. I was born during apartheid South Africa. They put 'mixed race' on my birth certificate. The city would not accept them, their love story so I was taken away, given up to a kind-hearted missionary family. I do not hate my mother. I never knew either of my parents. Laws, regulations, the powers that were replaced love, a mother's love. When I think about my mother now first you will find her, my mother with European blood, mostly German in her in the kitchen. She is baking a cake. I am licking the bowl out. It tastes like chocolate. It is for my birthday party. All my friends and cousins, family and family friends will be there but they are men and women dreaming about being found. I can't get back to him, my father, the garden boy who couldn't probably read or write. They found a sea of words and experiences in a rose garden filled with trees. Was my father a savage? My maternal grandfather probably thought so. He probably thought that my father was also a rapist. My mother was beautiful, sophisticated, elegant, and young. Much too young to have me. She was also mentally ill. There's an unbearable lightness to it when you're a sufferer of it in the world. People don't understand the stigma, you are hidden away like Mrs Rochester, Pinkerton's Sister, you drink like Jean Rhys, and you have a suicidal illness like Plath and Anne Sexton, you have love affairs. Brush the romanticism off them and become promiscuous. A she-wolf. And now all the time before I fall asleep, close my eyes I imagine my grandmother brushing my mother's hair before she goes to bed and wondering if my mother

70

wondered what happened to me and what was going to become of her. In my subconscious there are unstable, strained realities. Some are bipolar as there were inside my mother's head. The world does not seem to see me, understand me or accept me as a writer, poet, intellectual and rival to man. Where did help come from for my biological mother? She came from a wealthy Johannesburg family. Did she hold me when I was born or was I simply taken away? Did she understand what was happening around her?

'Can I read what you've written Bessie?' my doctor asks. He pushes his glasses up his nose. He is in his mid-thirties, young, young enough to be my son.

She feels as if she is defying gravity when she thinks about her son and where he is now. The doctor is as handsome as her son who was most probably now wandering throughout an unnamed city.

'I don't know if it makes much sense. I was a journalist in another world. Dimensions of truth always seem to lead me to a naked city. Doctor, you don't look as if you eat.'

The doctor smiles. 'I eat. But my day gets very busy. I usually have some tea and a sandwich or some fruit.'

'Yes, but you must eat something much more substantial than that.' I shook my head.

'How are you feeling today otherwise, Bessie?

'Tired. Pensive. The writing helps.'

'Hmmm. I see. It is good that you've found something to occupy your mind with. You see that is always good. You know that there is not much else we can do for people who suffer from your malady at the hospital.'

'Here's my notebook doctor. It is mostly fragments. It is almost as if my head is communicating to my heart but there's a filter. There's a switch in my brain. Do you understand what I'm saying?'

'Yes, I completely understand.' The doctor said without understanding. He leaned back against the bench and rested his hands on his knees. 'Do you miss those days at the newspaper?'

'Yes and no. Once in a while. All the time. Sometimes when I think about it I think about what I'm missing and sometimes I dream about it.'

'Tell me doctor do you have a wife.'

The doctor smiles. 'Yes, yes I do have a wife.'

'I don't believe you. If you had a wife, she wouldn't let you survive on fruit alone and a sandwich and tea for lunch.' The doctor smiled and then he began to laugh. The doctor laughed like a hyena. 'Heh-heh-heh-heh-heh.' He put his hand in front of his mouth as if he was coughing.

'Bessie, I think I will leave you now. I will take this with me, your notebook and read it. I encourage you not to be so pensive, not to think so much. And get as much rest as you can especially in the afternoons. It is good to rest. Good for the body. Good for the spirit. Keeps your spirits up. Good for the soul. Soup for the soul as the North Americans say. I read that in a book somewhere.' And since it was nearly Easter, I asked him if they would make pickled fish in this part of Africa, this part of the world and he said no. They ate a kind of fried fish, sometimes they dried it in the sun. He said it was delicious. His mother was still alive so she made it when there was a family function sometimes and his wife too. I turned my head as if I was telling the doctor a secret. The potatoes are hard. I can't eat this. So, I push it away on my plate. I drink my water. The nun pulls a face when she comes to collect my plate. I pretend I don't see. They always say we should eat everything on our plate and not leave a bite. The vegetables come in a watery broth that tastes like nothing but they say it is good for us. It will strengthen us.

'You won't be getting any fruit if you don't eat everything. Food is good for you.' I pretend I don't hear the nun. I rather pretend that I'm asleep. But I know that she knows I am only pretending. I feel sticky and hot. The sheets are pressed up against my skin. There is no air conditioning here.

I am making a supper. I am making a grown-up supper for my mother and me. I am cooking traditional. This is for a mother I have never met. She is wearing something out of The Great Gatsby as if she is a flapper. She wears a rope of pearls around her neck. She fingers every pearl as if someone is going to steal them from her. My table is unlike any table she's ever sat at. It is quite plain just like her wallflower daughter. Malay cuisine. She does not speak to me. She does not make eye contact with me. This is what those kinds of women were like in those days. The things she would say would kill me. 'This is too cold.' And she would make a face as if she was going to be sick. 'Take this away. I am not going to eat this. It's inedible.' Believe me there are some days I am happy I never knew her. Bright lunatic, bouncing off the walls there were moments when my moods were both electrifying and terrifying until I found myself in this country. Botswana and I immediately fell in love with it like I did with the name Maru. Outside seems to be a very good way of looking in. The earth bottom's out streaming, flowing. I taste the rain and swallow. Yes, even in Botswana it rains in the evenings when Africa is at her most beautiful. For wintering you need layers of clothes. Thoughts like who created the wounded in modern war. The parting gift from this prideful world to the hereafter. The fog has taken a lover. The wasteland that lies before and behind me, farming communities, families, lovers of Botswana where the light is all shiny and new. In the material world I go by the name of Bessie Head. Not even the important people read my books in South Africa even though I was published in London. I no longer fulfil that role or function here in this hospital. No longer wife, no longer mother, no longer journalist chasing after genocide, asking those tough questions. And so, I forget about the sun. When I think of suicidal illness, of the poetry that was written on the sometimes-brutal wonder of living and taking your last breath on this earth, I think about how Sylvia Plath wrote about the biblical Lazarus. And in spite of the men around her who thought they were worldlier than female poets and that she could never be worldly enough as if she was the first woman to even contemplate doing something like that (it had to come from a thought, a pure thought) and she did not fail. Everything after that was just a test that she passed, that was an achievement with flying colours. If I could become something much more than my disability, my infertility, the thread of alcoholism and addiction that ran throughout my family history on both sides of the family tree. If I could just become a sea of hands then I would become the winner who would stand alone.

When you say you don't love me at all

10

I am wearing ribbons in my hair. Today is my birthday and there are presents hidden with paper I can't wait to unwrap with trembling fingers. Children running around and screaming, kicking the legs of their chairs underneath the dining room table that is covered with the birthday spread. Death by cakes that is the price. I can taste it in my mouth, review it in my head, and feel it all sinister suspiciously in my blood. It is all coming back to me now. My mother, is she sad or glowering at my father across the room? Is he sad or the picture of health? I have eyes that can see. Can't the eyes of a child see everything? The butterflies are so pretty. I can't bear to tear through the wrapping. It's a belt but I smile. It's a hard smile. I don't care what Anita says although Anita is my best friend but I have known Lynne longer because her parents are friends with mine. My parents have always taught me that it is the thought that counts. I stare at the flowers. I am sharing everything with Eve, my sister. Today is her birthday also. On my fifth birthday my aunt, my mother's sister played host while my mother was in labour at the Livingstone with Eve. Everything since childhood has been down the road or a few minutes-walk, or an art not to fail or achieve, achieve, achieve, church, birth, high school, the park. There are other children here that I don't know. I don't speak to them. They are eating my cake. My mother is talking to them, asking about which school they go to, what grade they are in. She is wearing a pink dress with spaghetti-thin straps and sandals with heels. The dress has white polka dots on. She is much more animated with them than she is with me. She is smiling and laughing, asking them, these strangers in their party dresses who are parading across my mother's garden, oh-so-serious with their dark hair in long plaits if they are having a nice time, if they would like anything more to eat or to drink. If only she would pay attention to me. Everything about today is too bright, harsh, grating, working on my nerves. The sun for instance, a girl's laughter (who is older than me), the energy from all the traffic in the house, the line for dessert. My mother has the brightness of two suns. Her hair flows around her face, her perfume in a cloud and as her foot hits the sandal it makes a squelching, sucking sound. I am free to do what I want. So I choose to be alone. This is my day. Everyone else that I do not go to school with or play with in the afternoon are my mother's guests but all the girls seemed to have paired up with each other. They stand on the lawn looking bored, watching me the birthday girl and whispering secrets to each other. My sister, Eve is still too small to play or to understand what the day really means. The boys are playing a rough and tumble game of hide-and-seek. Then it is time for the ice cream. The adults are going to play a video, something suitable for the younger generation, a cartoon. I can never remember what happens to my father when all this 'playing' is going on. There are never uncles at my birthday. My mother is not in the kitchen with aunts and older cousins arranging pies, finger food for a small army of neighbourhood children or pouring wine in glasses for the adults mingling around the house. The uncles only come to drop their children off and then they are on their way again in their shiny cars pressing a creased note or a silver coin into my hand and kissing or rubbing the top of my head. I usually eat too much until my stomach hurts but there's the video. It is Looney Tunes, my favourite. I look around for my mother but she's not there. Eve is sitting too close to the television. I know that if I touch her, the golden child, she will yell and my mother would probably come running to see what is wrong and take me out in front of everyone. I feel lost and already I feel as if it is being stored up for a time when it will be of use, useful not to me but to other people.

15

Fifteen candles. There is nothing splendid about youth, growing older, feeling lost, unaccomplished and insecure. It just hurts, it hurts, it hurts. There is only the dreaming, the vision of escaping into marriage and having children that sticks. I am on that road of a poet who writes of madness and illness, the sweetness, the sweat of other people's lives. You wouldn't like me if you really knew me, knew who I was under lock and key, behind closed doors, poison flowing through my veins, pressure and stress touching the fragile core of me. The trophy doesn't feel, look real to me. But it is mine for a whole day and night before I have to return it. My name will be on it next year. For the first time in my life I feel the pulse of those two words put together, creative writing. I am set on another course, meeting Fugard, reading English novelists in the library during a break in the school day, winning a role in the house play but in all that rush it is still quite never enough. I am programming Adam, my brother. He has to be prepared for war. We can hear them at night in their bedroom behind the closed door. Maybe we would have been better off pretending that they were moving furniture around at night instead of fighting, gloves off, anything goes, bitterness flying through the air followed by mock defeat, tantrum after tantrum, hysterics and the glowing seed of madness. I'm not going to cry. I'm not going to cry. I'm not going to cry. This is what I write about in an essay for school. I stay up the whole night into the early hours of the morning writing it because I have left it for the last minute. I write about the holocaust. A young wife looking for her husband at a train station. It is different now from the beginning of the war when human beings were being transported like cattle, animals. These are survivors and she, the woman, the protagonist of my story, is looking for a family member or members. She imagines that he is still alive after Auschwitz and Bergen-Belsen. She is mad with grief. She is mad. But she believes because she has survived then so must he. I don't know how to end the story. In the end I decide on ending it with a flashback to the house they first lived in when they were married and the roses she grew at the back of the house. Living through the internal, warped struggle of pain is easier to bear if you have read stories of pain and mental anguish in books or the newspaper or watched television. I didn't call it 'female suffering' then. I didn't know what to call it. 'It' was just surrounded overwhelmingly with disbelief and a fog that for the most part was more than temporary and a saying that I chanted over and over again inside my head, giving it ample room to breath, to exist. No body can hurt as much as I do. There are some parts of me that are broken. My heart, my family, my father and the pieces that are broken are lost forever. Worst of all, humans make a habit of forgetting the best parts. They are irretrievable and dark. But on the screen in front of me I can piece them back together again. They fit nicely. For a while they, although the words might seem odd, they stay put and then I say that will do. It gives me a kind of therapeutic pleasure. The opposite of truth is looking at the theory of it all blindly and looking at the theory of it all feels like running backwards. The theory of husbands and wives breaking up and then getting back together again, going over that is the easy part. They reach a milestone in their relationship, some sought of agreement or consensus and when finally one reaches out to the other that spells the end for separation or divorce. But for the children instead of climbing hills merrily like other children their age, they will have to face mountains, climb the treacherous peak to get back to the start. They will also have to abandon the sides they choose but there was nobody to explain this to us, me, Eve and Adam when we were growing up. We didn't care. We made our own fun. We put on plays. We were each other's constant companions. We were happy. But the mechanism that kept our family together was going haywire. Our mother was a jumble of nerves. Our father, our hero and king was no longer the bright force in our lives that he once was. At night their bedroom door stayed shut and we couldn't even begin to imagine the personal torment and hell that he was going through.

17

The city reminds me of the sadness that I felt since I was a child. The Outsider, the loneliness, the ghost, the super rat catcher but that child is gone and in her place is a citizen of the world, a woman who needs to feel, to hear words of wisdom. A citizen who was taught that in everybody's life every moment of change is marked somewhat by pain, by a dream, by a faraway goal. The pages of my new journal are still fresh and new. I study them knowing that soon words will fill the pages, swim boldly, go where I have not gone before. Soon there will be words that will cauterise the page, leaving my head blank where it was once it was filled. There laid potential.

32

I have seen this in film, mental illness, the repercussions of hell, suffering and in the madness of men they are the creative thinkers, philosophers, called brilliant and genius, troubled in an unforgiving world. Those are the 'elite' names given to men. Did I need more explanation than that for the chronic mess I usually found myself in?

But I never knew the precise moment when I felt different or moved differently or articulated something with more bravado than I knew I had. But people that I knew and sometimes that I was close to knew that I was different and wasn't afraid to tell me so. Most times they made a joke of it. I am sure perhaps they did not mean to sound cruel, unkind or like a bully on a school playground but that is how I interpreted it. It still makes me nervous when I meet new people. When I have to make conversation, I always want someone to save me from myself. Do I howl when I laugh or snort with derision? Everything feels like the opposite of sublime, as if ants have got into the sandwiches in the picnic basket, as if I am covered in blood and people are staring. Female suffering is different from a man's rage and depression. They want to give their children what they did not have. They want to give their children what they longed for and wished for, what they desired as children and young girls before they became women and a picture, sometimes a mirror image of their own mothers. If a man is violent, a woman is emotional and sensitive. She has her own needs. For me to write was enough and for my mother it seemed that children and a large, spacious house to raise a family in was enough. But my father was not a violent man, a heavy drinker, a smoker, brutal towards my mother and me and my two siblings. He was warm, soft and cuddly like a teddy bear. He had brown eyes and made us all feel safe when we were growing up. He rested a lot. When he came home from school (he was a principal at a high school), I would watch him sleep from the doorway always waiting for him to wake up and catch sight of me. And I would wait for him to embrace me. I would never catch him embracing my mother because she hated public displays of affection. Not in front of the children, I could imagine she probably hissed under her breath so many times, too many for my father to count until he stopped doing it. At night my father would work on his doctoral thesis in his study. We were not to play near the closed door or disturb him. You can't imagine all the difficulties I have had to go through, the ghosts I have to put up with and the order and normalcy and simplicity I crave. What does snow feel, taste like? Like any wet, cold thing, like rain? The dogs are barking. They are going mad in the distance. There is something in his voice that annoys me, irritates me so I turn the television off. It must stay off. I am restless so I do what I know so well. I read. How far is it to the next hour? Why the overexposed, the challenges, mercies, points of departure, the roast chicken, vegetable soup welcoming me home? It is the dead of winter that I want; that I left behind in Johannesburg. It was the winter that toughened me up. Cold turning in the air, holding still in the middle of traffic facing off for their line of attack of the destitute huddled over fires under the highways and bridges and squatter camps where there are no wet leaves and butterflies. My sister seemed so cold and indifferent, aloof; she seemed to want to distance herself from us, the rest of the family as if she was made of brighter, harder, weightier stuff than the rest of us, as if it wasn't in her bloodline and the ladder of her genes to fail. We were weak, she was a saint. My reality for the better part of the day and sometimes the night was borderline, as if I was part of a tribe of people that time forgot in blue interiors. Swimming in a pool of blue; as if the blue had the same consistency as ink in my eyes, the blue skin of the swimming pool against my skin and of course, the pale blue school floating overhead like a ghost in a machine. Only here I felt safe amongst other schoolchildren and mothers, swimming instructors, lifesavers and fathers. Nobody could tell I was different. I was a nameless citizen. My limbs sank into the cool water as if I was sinking into hollows of warm sand. Home was a hot mess. Only in water could I escape from that fuss. Forget my brother was locked in rehab, forget my sister never

81

phoned to speak to me, forget that nobody ever phoned. That is what the writer works with – interiors, the dark and the lightest parts of it, the architecture of the formative years, objects around the writer working manners. What was left at the end or the beginning of the day was represented to me as light in a life force, a space to start from and a transition from a dream zone to a life lived in relative comfort. Away from the stresses of and from the different paths and roads I have taken, only I had access to the museum I had built up of all the negativity I had connected with and collected over my life experience. I wish it would be easier to explain things sometimes. This is what my mother does when she picks up a brush. A hairbrush, a toothbrush to put her 'other-face' on when she's off to church, a workshop at her church, to do service at the hospital, when she pushes off to a church meeting and then suddenly the love of God rises up in her when she dims her sweet pride, the rising panic and anxiety in the emotional screech of her hysterics as she makes waves all around us. She walks out with her heels clicking, glamorous and shiny, a smartly dressed Christian woman, her hair falling in dark brown curls around her face. Everything about her is soft, her clothes sticking to her figure, the flame of red on her cheeks, smelling like powder and scent, freshly washed blow-dried hair. Everything about me is hard, hardened by spent energy, by wasted time, by doing nothing, by sleep, by engaging my intellect and by asking myself, 'If my mother really loved me, why would she say those things? Does she hate daddy? Is God punishing me, us, the family and why?' This is memory and bitterness at work in the walking wounded. Ella's (she hasn't gone by that name for years) ghost sits at the foot of my bed staring at me with her long, sad, mournful face. I call her the 'genius behind the closed door'. I wait to hear for her footsteps in the dark. She keeps me company in the early hours. When dawn comes with the light filtering through the thin curtains, I turn around to look for her, but she is never there. Usually I am the talkative one and she listens. I mean with the state that she is in; all she can do is stare and wonder really what has brought the two of us together and who sanctioned 'it', this relationship. I am reading her books. I want to read all of them and push myself to get through it all. All the real-life episodes, the real madness of her, her lovers, her experiences, the death of her son, separation from her daughter and the alcoholism but what I really want to ask her is, how do you love, how do you fall in love. Is it always an experiment? Does it always feel unnatural and disturbing when the person you're in love with leaves you, is someone always going to be hurt and the will the one on the receiving end of that hurt, that intense feeling of rejection and pain relive it in recurring flashbacks. I have many questions and I hope to find the answers to them in her books, the genius in her books. Ella, I want to say, help me. Help me to understand the cause and effect of the love affair. Alone with all the difficulties of illness. What does that mean? To long for company, the smell of rain, to live and breathe solitude. Birds singing, the wind's song and the sun disappearing behind clouds, cool breeze, father exercising, also writing, and pensive and mother resting in the quiet of the afternoon. Thinking of how I came to be in this world, alone, with my books and my writing, me with my sad, brown eyes and dark hair, brittle soul and serious nature. Now look at me. Look at how far I have come. Look at how far I still have to go. The obstacles and challenges of my youth are no longer facing me. Over time things will change. I will become more set in my ways. Discontent my middle name, peculiar, peculiar, peculiar, even more so at 32, with my life hanging precariously in the balance, no ring on my finger. Was it all worth it? The bullying mother, the bullies on the playground, the matron and the captain hissing under their breath to mop the floor at the Salvation Army, clear the tables, wash the dishes, pack the crates, unpack them with the perishables going into the storage room, the meat going into the fridge. Even then I was living in a dream world. Imagination, the consolation prize, always under the illuminating spell of imagination, gripped by its fierce call and something was loosed in me. Johannesburg and Port Elizabeth, always two cities rising up to meet me head on, a crash test dummy set on a collision course with nowhere else to go but to meet the world in a thin line with hope put aside. A dummy that knew the final outcome would be misery. I would wash the crates. Wash them out with a hose, dry them with a damp cloth and then stack them up against a wall outside. They would be filled later that day with food from Woolworths. Was I happy doing this? No, not really but in a way, it comforted me. I was around people and that had to count for something. Something in me expanded. I wasn't that solitary figure that stood out in assembly. A stick figure, all arms and legs, awkward, who could hardly speak, open her mouth, stand her ground. I was around people who were like me, estranged from family, homeless rejects that had a low opinion of themselves, no sense of self-worth, who wanted to give of themselves but didn't know how. Somehow being around people like that made me a kinder, more sincere version of myself. I spent nearly a year at the Salvation Army and before that a few months at a shelter. Looking back on those times, I can sense it must have been a very frightening time for me but it went by in a flash and now I have adventures, poignant and sad, funny and wise to write about. The people I have met have become like well-known characters in stories, liked, loved very much and hated. I feed on their loss, my suffering and the world that I saw in their eyes that was launched into the space around them. And then there was my world. Sometimes I soared and there were other days I didn't. Those were the days when I took liberties with my neurotic female sentiment. When I preferred to slide under the covers, addicted to the warmth and comfort. No addiction is kind, I tell Ella. Did she just move her head in agreement, in my direction? She, of course I have figured this out now, is just here to guide me. I understand all I have to do is talk. Whispering will suffice. I don't have to be loud. What does it take to be a writer, to write? Her eyes seem to say you'll soon figure that part out elegantly. There is no need for you to be so superstitious but then again, those are clearly my words, not hers. I move backwards in time. I move to childhood. 'Age before beauty,' snigger, snigger, sniggering behind my back and then I am on the steps, on the way to class, my cheeks burning. I am turning red but no one can see. I am safe for now because no one can see. Tonight, they were fighting again. Although they closed their bedroom door, I could still hear them, father as docile as a pet and mother screaming. What they usually fought about was money. If my mother loved me, she didn't say it. But was it all worth it, one tragedy and one adventure, one unfortunate discovery of the cruel and dangerous world in my life after the other? Yes, yes and yes. Overwhelming loneliness. What does that mean? First you succumb to it and then you must overcome. I take long walks up deserted streets, through crowds, the lunch rush in the financial hub of Johannesburg. I talk animatedly to Ella, as if I must make up for lost time, for something that I must still gain. She does not smile. But tonight, she has turned away from me as if she knows something that I do not know. This is a loneliness that I must bear. It is my burden. How can I refuse it, refuse kismet? I am a grown woman, not a child yet I still feel as if there is something of the child about me. When will that change? When will sensibility start creeping in, a feminist intuition? On maturity, illness, mothers and daughters I have this to say. If I can see from where I am standing next to my bedroom door, (this is ajar because I left it like that) through the window made of lines

85

of yellow light, shiny parts at my front door and stare into the face of a stranger, what would I see, their meeting, their eyes, intent, winter, my own washed-out or ill reflection depending on what day of the week it was? Would I see a vision or feel a change flicker and dance within the usual outspoken me, would we make commonplace conversation? Would I give my peace of mind away as I make the stranger a cup of coffee so hot that steam rises in puffs almost like white smoke in a glance? The stranger never smiles at me. I am just a poet and a writer feeling the air near my hands, pushing those buttons, dreaming a life half-lived in silence with prescriptions and medicine. This is what it has come to, the bride of kismet and the cornerstone of all illness, a weak link in the system on the take. This is my home, my ending, my silver lining, my ray of hope, me bright with the knowledge, expectation and insight of the oftentimes unbearable energy of illness. It makes a mute and deaf clown of me. A clown who is very bad at telling jokes, getting laughs, falling over his oversized clown shoes, his nose a shiny red like a siren. I am not doing what I am supposed to, following the order that nature has set out for me. In the cold, cold night when my skin tastes like salt, when the street lamp glows in the dark, when stripes of shadows seem to win me over to sleep to the light that hits falling angels. I think of bottles littered on a field, the stamina they give a man, roads into madness, softness and sanctuary and I am reminded of the stranger at my door, the silver in his hair and beard. How we both are cast out into the black, into loneliness to settle into its purity, its season, its ritual, its intense quiet out there. With the eyes of a child I watch the pilgrimage of the blue veins beneath the surface of your skin. Exposed to light and air they seem delicate, their pangs healthy and swimming pale, breathing down my neck. Clouds, floating mentors, they're stiff illuminations as I fall into the ill flowers crushed by air and days and here in the dreamlike blue is courage melting the hearts of stone of the broken, the weak, the darkness of humanity and what of silence in rooms? And when I fall into the memory of you sitting at my table, your tongue bittersweet. Pure is this sense of being, of belonging to someone, of being something greater than the sum of your parts. Is this false like the view of the union of the moon and sun and earth from this world? Woman as Muse never leave me or else I will always be wintering, waiting in a sense to be washed clean, to return to you as a woman in the flesh, an epic childhood packed away. Once you were everywhere I went, I called you 'mother', said 'please' and 'thank you'. You gave me these words, a hard and determined brother, Adam, a sister, Eve, a soft girl. If the world is not my home then it is only a point of no return until I stop for death meeting eternity. As butterflies transform in winter like I do, do they say like I do, 'I'm helpless, please heal me?' before they pierce your soul. I hated school so I imagined fairytales in class and there I found even you. So I became an avid collector of words. All I wanted was peace. When Eve went away to study and then later to work, she did not promise to write or stay in touch or phone. It was as if she had disappeared off the face of the earth or had gone underground to another time, another place, another city, the Cape. I know now what the ocean's life must feel like, what it must fear but the hours give me courage. It tells me that there's love, passion, empathy in my blood even the silence in profound madness, even in the weeping for my loss of that brave little thing, Eve, Evie. I did not mean to end up here. In my tales that soft girl, Eve, the favored daughter, her skin the color of health, is usually in a dress or a skirt with an African print, always hovering in the background as if she had no voice, as if she had nothing of importance to say. Instead she's building fences (taking pictures for her photography course), mending burnt bridges in a moment and in the next building an empire of art. In the land of the living she moves like a ghost with a consummate ease from one room to another (yes, I've found a word for it). She's moved away from home, where the child inside her died. Eve replaced that 'child' casually with flowers, a hundred material things, bottles of scent; books filled with meaning traced the emptiness in her soft heart. I was left with tears blinking like diamonds in my eyes.

Leonard and Virginia Woolf, the honeymoon

I like the way you move in that dress. Here, let me help you with that. He started to kiss her. Brushing his lips against her warm mouth, until she began to respond to him, trembling in his arms. Holding onto him, then hugging him hard as if she would never let him go. She licked her lips, opened her mouth, and bit his bottom lip seductively. Not sure where do you want to go with this. All the way then. She stepped out of her fashionable brogues. She had to sit on the bed to do this, untie her laces. She nodded. Stepped out of her dress. Lifted her slip over her head. Smoke. I need to smoke. She looked away, back to him again, standing there, feeling slightly absurd in his socks. She made him feel like a rambling teenager. Youthful. Already his hair was dishevelled. Hers was unkempt. Quintessential bed-hair, he thought to himself. He kept on regarding her. Her beauty. Her vulnerability. The fact that now she was telling him to undress in front of her. He undid his belt buckle first and loosened his tie. Running his hands yet again through his hair, and was thinking what her breath would sound like when she was close to orgasm, or in his arms, as he touched a loose strand of her hair, tucking it behind her ear. He wanted to caress every part of her. Her physicality, both the locus of her internal and external locus of control. He thought of the very first conversation they had ever had, the very first moment he had ever met her eyes, told her that he loved her. She made him feel shy. She called him sweet. She called him gentle. The men in his social circles asked about her, but he was always vague. Never wanting to reveal what he truly felt for her. Would she love every minute of it, of their hours together, would she love him, accept his desire for her? He wasn't 40-years-old anymore. They had the entire afternoon, the evening. Hours. She looked at him then. Their eyes met. Recognition, at last, the man thought to himself. Leonard and Virginia together again. The nomad and the recluse together again. You're perfect. You're extraordinary. Truth. You're beautiful. Now, you show me. Show me your love, Adeline Woolf. I'll be gentle with you. You exemplify womanhood and femininity. Tell me about your wounds, Adeline. She looked away then. Afterwards, we can go for a long walk. You'll come to love Sussex just as much as I have. I have so many plans in development. For you, Adeline. For us. Just think! We have the rest of our lives to think things through, understand each other, grow in love and faith like the mustard seed. She began to kiss his neck. He put his hand on the nape of her neck. I love you, Mrs Adeline Woolf. We'll do whatever you like. You'll write. I even have a name for our printing press. Hogarth. What do you think? She sat up then. The woman sat up in bed. You're cold. Let me close the window. He turned around at the sound of her laughter. Lovely, foolish, awkward and frightened little girl. A good laugh at my expense, he said while stroking her pale thigh. She leaned her head into his shoulder. The woman kissed his shoulder. Then she rested her head against the pillow as he entered her. Hours. They had hours. Hours to fill with love and lovemaking, tenderness and vertigo. Are you wet, Mrs Woolf? Are you the happiest you've ever been, my love, my love, my love? Did I hurt you? I would never dream of hurting what belonged completely, and utterly to me, you know that, my love? She turned to look at him again. The relationship had been consummated. They were husband and wife now and belonged completely, and utterly to each other for eternity. Into the hereafter, and beyond the sunset of the page. Until their bones turned into fossils like the dinosaurs in the museum, until Edinburgh fell, until the moors turned green because of climate change, and global warming. Until the end of time they would remain here, in this room, praising the physicality of their bodies. Never losing sight of their childhood fondness of each other. We are one now. Together against the war, your stepbrothers. Leonard W. whispered in her ear. I would do anything, anything, anything for you Virginia, my love. Thief, thief, thief with every breath you take, with all the hours you give me, with every moment of your beating heart you thrill me. Wife, he said as he stroked Adeline Virginia Woolf's hair. Tucking a stray curl behind her ear and subtle intimacy. Heat. He could feel the heat between her legs. Wife. Who would have thought that he would have captured Adeline's heart after all? Bringing her here to Sussex. Living and working here away from London had been the right decision. She was far away now from the memories of her married artist sister Vanessa Bell, and her dead brother Tobey, and especially that rough-and-tumble Bloomsbury Group, somehow both sexually inept and worldly men and women, searching for meaning and purpose through art. Through their art. Whether it be writing, or painting and drawing, or putting on sketches to amuse themselves, drinking coffee in the evenings before retiring to bed. Leonard would not call having a promiscuous lifestyle and love affairs, men meeting up with men, women meeting up with women, men and women meeting up with each other's art. Making love for fun was not what he considered 'art'. But that was his private opinion, and he had adored Virginia, always, and her siblings, and the fact that she had made room in her heart for him sent him into spasms of pleasure as he thought of her climaxing, her body trembling beneath him, their eyes meeting again, and again, and again. He knew that she had never known such unconditional love and acceptance from a man, any man before. Not even her father. Her mother had died so young. She was sleeping now. Happy wife. Devoted husband.

Vanessa Bell, the other genius sister

Oldest friend, loving sister, this is goodbye. I'm journeying once again into the wilderness, but this time without you. I promise you that I won't think of you every step of the way as I did before. I promise you that there'll be no declarations of love this time around. You're so obsessed with the lens, with the camera. You're in love with everybody, that's your kind of education, your kind of hardworking-philosophy. You're bird with song. You say that you love her, so love her like family, your mother. One word from you, one false alarm, changed everything about our past. Old friend, so, this is goodbye. This time next year you'll be married, and I'll never hear from you again. I pray that you'll have poetry in your life, stories, narratives, concepts, reminders of concepts, life in perspective, in context, sipping on Saint America's supernatural provision. And words take on a life of their own. Let your wife shop for clothes, and when she's pregnant let her shop for maternity-wear, your hands will drift across the waterfall of her dark hair. The path you have to go is ecstasy, touch her restless soul, and then let her touch yours, wonder boy, genius boy. You're Zambia, Burkina Faso, Ghana, and the Ivory Coast. You, Clive Bell, only win when you hear her talk in her sleep. There's a shore she has to reach to get to you, whenever you close your eyes. Your sea is beautiful this time of year, the origin of your universe, baby galaxies are at rest, space is expanding back into time closer, closer. It contracts to a certain point, and returns to time, energy and matter. The flesh is just the absolute beginning of your life, your love's tragedy, illustrations of science. Sister, I wish for a parade of family life for you. You will be most thorough when it comes to your love. I was all wrong for you from the start, could never make you happy, my emotional damages would have become your emotional damages, at night I sleep with Alba at my side, and you sleep like the gospel, the spiritual racing through all of your nocturnal molecules holding the knock, search and obey through faith and action, my old love. Your children will be your prize. Faith is risk not yet seen, a standing conviction of things not seen. I was saved through your grace, the mask that you use, the taste of red, red wine. You did not choose me after all. I have Bloomsbury, Paris, and all this madness war. The end of August. Life is beautiful (the writing life). Aren't glaciers even beautiful, the rush of winter in the trees, birdsong in the clear of day and the clarity of the sensibility of all of them. But writing, the book stuff is something else. It is mixed with the salt of the earth, blue, sharp and intensely felt light. It grounds you and smells like dust up in the air, books that have to be launched, poets-in-the- making. July and August have passed into that ancient otherworldliness called ether and newspapers and research, writing, and study. I don't answer the voices sometimes. I ignore the hallucinations. It's all a part of life, my life. Sister, nothing compares to you since you took your love away. Not the pale sea, not Sussex. And the only things that I seem to have on my mind is that I don't have enough time in the world during the day to write, to perfect the craft of writing, the art of it. So, wish-fulfilment has been on my mind, that and everything else that is happening to 'the people of the south', the people in South Africa, the vulnerable. Everything is fleeting, including your youth. At the heart of it all we're all poets. But most of all I'm frightened of the wild, of the wilderness disappearing. I am mourning the loss of our mountains, and rivers. What are your answers on how to sell a book and save the world at the same time? And I'm frightened all the time. Frightened of being an invisible person, an invisible woman for all of my life, or am I forgetting myself again. Fear and anxiety rise up in my masculine throat. The voices say that I am mad, that I will never get a man, and he will never trust my judgement. The loneliness wells up inside of me. I think of the reality of my dreams, and nightmares. The men that I telephone, who accepted my friendship when I was in my early twenties, who do not return, who have stopped returning my calls. Sister, shy away from me. The voices worship, and adore me. They do, they do, they do. They're fierce creatures when it comes to the burden, and care of loving me, heavenly when they play my love songs on repeat. Video did really kill the radio star. Fear is what I hold dear. Anxiety is what I cherish. I am volcano lover versus oil on my hands. I am devilish. I am exquisite. I am poet. I am lake. Sometimes I go where the mood takes me. Sometimes I am numb with cold, the freezing to death because of the air in my room, salt, and light, and energy on the forsaken summer breeze, and I think of my arms, and legs as I do branches. I need you, Vanessa. I smell like a forest of trees. Ancient and cool, like driftwood spat out of the cold sea. The men I once loved are decades older, and I still long to be in their arms, to be in their bed. I search the internet for online literary journals in Scandinavia, because the voices tell me that I am something of a poet. I have sorrows on my mind, the colour blue, fish fingers on my plate heavy with apricot chutney, chapped lips, a greasy egg breakfast. Vertigo goes to my head. In modern life and times, I watch Joel Osteen on the television. Afterwards the television evangelist Joseph Prince. They give me the good news that I want to hear. And yes, yes, I mustn't waste my pain. All I want you to do is to remember me. I don't want a lover, I just need a friend, like I need sobriety, like I need a man in my life. Women don't want to be my friend. They rather treat me unkind. Laugh at me behind my back. I will always remember you, you, and you. How you said I was behaving, like I had been misbehaving, not taking my medication. How you spoke to me as if I was unwell. That I needed to be treated for the depression again, or something, or something else this time around. I won't forget your words, or your fiancé with her hair like black silk touching her waist. Like our dead mother. Like our dead mother. I have stopped loving you. I am not in love with you anymore. I would be a fool. I would be the insecure coward. You win traitor. You've got the girl now. You've got that woman on your arm. You made a fool out of me. Never replied to my flirting. Perhaps I was lovesick, traitor. You're yesterday, traitor. You're suffering. Traitor. You are kismet, milk-fed, champagne snorting through your nose at the parties, and social gatherings that you go to with that girl on your arm. I give you my blessing. Clive Bell, marry my sister. Grasp her in your arms as flowers. As if you will never let her go. Modern sister, you let me go, go. I really wish you would smoke. Light up that joint, fall asleep with marijuana in your bone season, but you won't. You won't think of snorting cocaine up your nose. You'll drink sherry, but half-heartedly, just to join in with the rest of your in-crowd. You're still as popular as you ever were in high school. All the girls, no matter what their age, they all fall for you. They are all in love with you. I feel split right down the middle, because of you traitor, part of me calls you vulnerable, part of me remembers the intimacy of our conversations. I long for a bowl of black olives. They are salty and they're all sanctioned for me. My blues. I long to spit the stone out, like you spat me out, traitor, as if I was the criminal in this narrative. I'll write a book about you one day, see if I don't. I swear on my father's wheelchair, I swear on his life, I will, I will, I will. I won't call you sweetheart. I won't call you friend. Vanessa, you took your love away. I forgive you darling sister. I need you Vanessa, but you don't need me. Torn between Clive and your fragile sister's desperation. It has been so lonely without you here. Lonely tears fall. I am caught by the ways of the loneliness of the river.

The curious language of Laura, Lynn and Peter

Laura

I was the angel. The good one. I was the one with the children and the husband. The glowing mother. The successful writer. The novelist. Not Lynn. I have a home. I was the one with the family. I was the lucky one. I am thirty something or other now. I am a daughter, a sister, wife, and a mother. An independent woman who was taught early on to love her body for the bright translations it offers up to me, 'me', at a moment's notice. My body does not belong to me anymore. It belongs to winter. That adrenaline rush. That fight/flight. I needed to have proof of the stars. So I reached out to the clouds during the day. I beckoned sunlight. I measured its weight. Felt its shape with my fingers. Found a place for it. I needed to say to the universe give me the moonlight. Let it shine its spotlight on me. Let the rain wash my sins away. It's cold. It's so cold. I can hardly feel my feet. My hands do not belong to me anymore. They belong to another world. Another king. I gravitated towards its foliage. My mother raised two girls but in the beginning of mum and dad's marriage there were whispers, issues of infertility. It was something never spoken about. It's winter. Winter clothes lost in translation. The throne that is called a tree's shiny leaves. I let its itchy arms hold me close. Bring closure to the cold-heartedness of winter. The winter guests of leaves, of lighthouses, of foreclosure. Then, only then will I happily toil this earth for you, for Peter, for Lynn, for my children, until the end of the world. Until death comes for me or eternity. I'm not tired yet. I want to stay up and watch the sun rise. Waiting for the future. Waiting for ghost matter. Plants to grow in the earth that I've toiled for you. Putting my heart aside.

Lynn

Dear Peter, friend and lover, I miss you. You slipped or fell all beautiful and original folds of you through my fingers in the city I fled from as a girl. Johannesburg. I write about Johannesburg's people from memory. That love song and mad dance of pollution, climate change, global warming. I don't want you in my head anymore. Clearly you've moved on. You're married. Your wife's expecting. Your life is perfect. I still think about you. I still write about you. Love poems to myself.

Laura

A flood always comes with change. Religion is golden. It is another far-off city. I'm a Christian so I can't do that. I don't smoke cigarettes because my body is a temple, and stars always seem to silence me. It's in me to find a voice for them. I can't wish ill on another person. Can't wish revenge on them. That it's best served cold. All I can do is believe in the sweetness of human life. The best of humanity. I know that I am not responsible for your wings. For you being lost in translation. You're beautiful anyway. We're Christians but when we're flying off the handle we're also sisters, Daughters, losing our religion. I almost inherited the rain when it came. Childhood is brief. It is making me grow smaller and smaller. I see the two of us, Laura and Lynn eating chicken and ribs in a restaurant, celebrating someone's birthday in photographs. Posing, Laughing our heads off. Our childhood was brief but it was brilliant. I showered your face with kisses. The backyard was the wilderness filled with tigers and snakes. Wild tigers, and poisonous snakes that we had to catch. Pretend to kill. You're always giving me a speech now. Lecturing me on my potential. I always say I love you at the end of our conversations through the whirring loophole of the telephone. I feel this is the last city. I am not going to move house again from here. This is my last house. My last renovation. The last time I will paint these walls. My last psychiatrist. My last psychologist. And when I had the children, it was the last time that I was ever going to be alone. Be myself. I was now supposed to be a responsible adult. I had brought life into the world. I always found sanctuary in winter. Midwinter.

She could hear him singing and this made her smile. It made her happy to think that she had done that. Brought that smile to his face.

'Say hello.' He said.

'Hello.' She smiled back at him.

'Show don't tell.' Her stroked her arm and kissed the nape of her neck.

'Isn't it supposed to be ask don't tell.' She closed her eyes.

'Something like that.' He opened the newspaper. His glasses perched at the end of his nose.

'Does this mean we're a couple? We tell each other everything, don't we.' she turned her head to admire his profile.

'Togetherness for a man means altogether something different to a woman.' He turned the page to the business section

'Always? How sure are you about that?' She sat up and brushed the hair out of his face.

'You need a haircut, darling.'

'Yes, whatever.' He answered in return.

'You're not listening to me.' She sat up and put the pillows behind her back.

'Oh, I am very sure that having a relationship means different things to a woman than it does to a man. Do you like my sister?' Laura crossed her arms when she looked at him. She knew he wasn't going to give her a straight answer.

'Yes, yes I do. What's not to like? You love her. You like her. I like her too. I think that she is very nice.' Peter never looked up from the newspaper but he was paying attention to her now.

'Nice. Do you think she is beautiful? A lot of people think that she is beautiful.'

'You're beautiful, Laura, and I'm with you.'

'No, I'm not. Not like that. I don't have a magazine look, Peter.'

'You're good enough for me.' He leaned over and kissed her on her cheek.

'Petey, then again not what a woman wants to hear.'

'Okay, she's beautiful. Why won't you believe that you're beautiful too? This is what I don't like about you. You're so insecure sometimes, you know and you don't have to be. You just don't.' He brushed his hand through his hair. It brought a smile to Laura's face every time he did that. He looked so handsome. It was times like these that she thought to herself that she really didn't deserve him.

'Peter, I always want you to be honest with me. Promise me, that you will always be honest with me, always.'

'Laura,' Peter sighed. 'I'm not going to marry your sister. I'm going to marry you because I am in love with you.'

'Let's go for a walk. I have all this bunched up nervous energy.' She got out of the bed and stood in front of the mirror looking at her reflection. 'Say that again.'

'Say what, love?'

'Say that you're going to marry me, babe.'

'Okay, if it will make you happy. I'm going to marry you. Besides I don't feel like walking anywhere today. I just don't feel like it. The walk. Let's put it off. Let's stay here instead for the rest of the afternoon. I'll make us coffee and croissants.'

'I think that I would like that very much. You making me breakfast. Promise me breakfast in bed for a lifetime and I'm yours.' Laura smiled at him, then looked back at her dishevelled appearance in the mirror.

'Anything for you, sweetheart.'

Laura lifted Peter's shirt up over her head, pulled it over her shoulders.

'Don't disturb me for the next hour or so I want to finish the pages I started yesterday. I love inhaling you.'

'You're the best thing that happened to me Laura.'

'And don't you forget it.' She winked at him.

Lynn

I am the last city, the sanctuary. The language of snow in Johannesburg is tired now and, I am tired of the layers of winter clothing. I just don't want Laura to resent me now for the burden that I have become in her life. Of course, Laura stopped writing seriously when the second child arrived. A boy and then when I got sick there was a girl and a boy and Peter and then me. She never brought the children with her when she came to visit me at the hospital. Sometimes Peter would come with her but he would hover. He would say a quiet, stiff, forced 'hello,' and then speak to the men. Smoke with them as they stood outside on the patio. Even when it rained he would do that. Laura would say comforting things and apologise for not bringing the children who were in their teens by now. We would talk about the same things, mill around them. The children, Peter's work. Peter was a director. Something important. Some high profile job that I could never understand really. Laura was always very happy to see me. She always bought me bitter chocolate. I was the last city. I was the city she was never going to leave. The walls that she was going to leave the same color. We spoke about that brick wall of clinical depression in full sentences. I asked her to stop coming, and then I asked her to stop bringing Peter with her. I didn't want anyone to feel sorry for me especially him. I loved him, but I also loved him like a sister loves a brother. He was the brother I never had but that was before they got married. When Laura first got married it wasn't like before. Things had changed and I had to get used to it. Couldn't just pick up the phone and call her like I used to. We couldn't hang out and chill with each other. Go on holidays with each other.

'Don't come. I'm damaged. I don't want you to be around me, Laura. I think the reason I'm like this is because of the relationship mum had with dad. Did our parents love each other?'

'Yes, of course mum loved dad, and dad loved her in his own way.'

But Laura could never see it from my view. It didn't end there. Sometimes when she came to visit we used to fight. I used to fight with her. Ask her not to come anymore because I was so ashamed. Shamed that my life was a mess. Shamed that I was unsuccessful. That I didn't have those kids. That husband. Peter, and the children were her whole life.

'Why wouldn't I want to come? Lynn, you're my sister. My only sibling. We have this connection. We always have. I have to help you through this now. It could even be in my family. Think. My children. Your niece. Your nephew. In our genes.'

'Oh, Laura. Life takes. I could never get married now. You know that. After the depression, how can I love anyone, fall in love again. I'm no good to anyone. No good to you.' Then Laura would take my hand in hers and squeeze it until I couldn't feel it anymore. She will turn to me and say, 'It's all that medication you're taking. You're just not yourself. You see, when you come home with me and Peter, the children, things will be different.'

I would hold onto her before she left. Peter would come over and call me 'sport' or 'kiddo'. 'Everything alright here, with the two of you.' He would always say and I would smile and kiss his cheek like a sister would kiss her brother. I couldn't make out who he was anymore. The man that I had slept with was not the same man who called me 'sport', and 'kiddo'.

Peter

I am the unknown. Yes, I slept with Lynn. It would break Laura's heart if she ever found out but Lynn was so different before she got sick. She was exciting. Beautiful. She was dazzling, and so was her personality. The first time I met her she was laughing at something Laura had told her and she looked at me and smiled. I smiled back. I think Laura saw something between us because later she said that Lynn had that electrifying effect on everyone she met. It was like I was sleeping with Laura's twin. She held my hand in the kitchen. Came up behind me and took me by surprise. I looked at her open face. I knew what she wanted me to do. Every time I looked at her I knew she wanted me to make a move. She wanted me to make that telephone call. I know what to call her now. She's emotional, her tantrums hysterical. She's unstable. There were flags. Looking back there were conversations. Life hurts. This painful struggle. I can't live anymore she said once but everybody says that at some point in their lives. I didn't take her seriously. Nobody did.

Dear Husband

I am a little girl again when I see my mother kiss another man on the lips. I only ever saw her kiss my father on the lips. This man's name was Uncle. My mother promised me a book, and a bar of chocolate, and any flavor of ice cream. I waited in the car. The door opened and my mother embraced Uncle while he ran his hands up and down my mother's back. I remembered Christmas. Of how much my father adored my mother and would do anything to make her happy. It was really my father who taught me how to be a good wife.

'Stop. Someone who knows us might see.' she said. My mother blushed. She was standing on the steps of Uncle's house.

'Who will see? The child can't see, and in any case she won't understand.' Uncle said messing up my mother's hair, and her lipstick.

'Children are bright. Children are curious about everything. I don't know. Well, all I know is that my daughter is bright as well as curious.'

'Children are curious at her age about love?'

'Is that what this is?' I pretended not to see but strained to hear every word.

'Love.' Uncle said again. 'When will you come and see me again?'

'When he is working or away on business or at a meeting? When I run errands, or go shopping?'

'Do you have to bring her? This is my territory.'

'Yes. She is my daughter. She has beautiful manners.'

'I am not her uncle. She called me Uncle once.'

'She is a very polite child. She is also a very bright child.'

'She looks at me funny. I just don't like the way she looks at me when you leave.'

'She's too young to understand.'

'Are you in love with Uncle, mother?' I asked my mother when she got in the car. She didn't say anything for a very long time. Uncle went inside the house, and closed the door. I looked across at her face. She had a dreamy look on her face. She had closed her eyes. She took my hand, her eyes still closed and said to me, 'You are too young to understand this. The effort of love, of having a family, running a household, having daughters, having a husband, being hurt, and falling in love. A man who understands you like no other. I love your father but there are things in this world that you will only understand when you are older. When you become a young woman. Do you know how to keep a secret? Well, today you are going to learn how to keep one.'

We never spoke about it again because I believed her. I believed her because she was my mother, and I loved her, and I thought she was a saint. Well only ghosts can have read lips, have flashbacks from childhood, and have the remains of the hours spent with the love of their life. I thought perhaps it would be best if Uncle would go on a long journey to Africa to shoot lions. If only a lion would eat him. Swallow him whole. He would be in the lion's belly while I decided his fate. Perhaps he would wake up one day and not love my mother so much. I would make a wish, and sleep with my leather-bound bible under my pillow. I was not an adult. I was a child. I already knew what 'sleeping around' meant. I already knew how red-faced babies were made.

She said I was her daughter, and so I kept her secret. Hitler came and went, and so did the war and still I kept her secret.

Love, where are you? Are you in heaven? Are you in a paradise or where the souls of the lost and found find each other? Have you found yourself in the afterlife, or the hereafter of the astral plane? Or like me are you a ghost. Do you find yourself haunting the places, and the people that you knew before the war? Do you find yourself riding trains with cows, trains that were once used to transport people to the camps? Once you were a boy making model airplanes, flying a kite on a hill, tobogganing down a snowy slope in winter, building a man made out of snow. I will never feel heat. You and I will never feel brave anymore. Brave in the sense of facing the world out on our own. There is too much golden light here. Do you have eyes to see? Do you have hands to feel? In a normal reality you would have to strike a balance, but it wasn't like that during the war, or even before war broke out. I don't have a life outside of writing books, and reading them. For a long time I have felt both this internal, and external struggle as a writer. What is my purpose? What have I sacrificed? The answer to both of those questions is everything.

I bit into the love of it all. Into the love story. Nothing has tasted sweeter. Seemed more significant to me in my life. I bit into the story. The bittersweet history of the pomegranate. You had your testimony. I had mine. Your laughter has an extraordinary soul. You are perfect. Always were. I study your profile. I contemplate you. Perhaps children or a child in the future. Every illusion. Sacrifice. Our growing intimacy. You are mine. All mine. All mine to worship. To compete against. To share my joy with when it comes to that. You are my constant companion, and advisor. Everything has fallen away. The death of everything. The mud season. Dead rotting leaves. Violence, and brutality in nature. You are as big as the sky. You are noble, serious, kind, warm, sincere, funny, and sweet. I can share my world with you. You are beautiful with your tangledwreck of hair. I am always aware of you in your absence. The history of the universe's big personality began with you.

Startled out of its reverie. Refreshed, audacious. It was a novelty. Everything is possible now. You have put your mark on me, this ring. I have put my stamp on this relationship. Running your household. You are nonchalant. You, the anthropologist in this relationship. You the photographer as clairvoyant. When people talk of the holocaust, they will not talk of us. There were thousands. There were millions. There were those that escaped. There were those that remained behind. You could play the piano. You loved jazz records. You loved me. I have a library to keep me warm now instead of a body whose face is streaked with tears and that smells of the fumes of gas. It is not winter. It is not winter yet. It is the same old same old where I am right now. I am in heaven. I am in paradise. I can feel the sun on my skin even though it is winter. My head is filled with dreams. I have goals when I step out into traffic. I do not sleepwalk anymore.

I do not have bad dreams when I have the memory of you to keep me company. It has been a whirlwind, I mean after the war. Getting to grips with life, with living, with putting behind that god awful, hellhole of a war. Getting to grips with the ones who were left behind. Everybody has to start at the beginning again. Put down roots no matter how hard coming to terms is. Everybody has a story. I have listened to many stories. I love looking at the stars. It is beautiful up there now. No war. No bullets. No Nazis. No guns breaking skulls.

No aching heartbreak in your throat being locked away as you inhale and exhale after walking away from your loved ones. No soldier soldiering on. I wish we could turn back time. To our wedding day. To our first kiss. Our first dance. The very first moment we met. I get all misty-eyed. You were a successful pianist. Perhaps I should have believed in you more.

You loved your chicken. Now when I look at chicken all I can see is you. I can see your face. Your hands on the lids of the pots on the stove. You spreading crumbs on the table. You never complained about my cooking. You never complained about anything really. Now all I can see is you eating my chicken, praising my skill in the kitchen, and I just looked at you, and I smiled to myself. You took my hand and kissed it. Life was perfect then. Life before the onset of the war. You loved your meat and potatoes. You boasted once that you were a meat and potatoes man, and I said that you loved chicken as well. Men were either meat potatoes men or men who loved chicken. We always argued about that but never about Hitler.

Scottie and Zelda Fitzgerald

'Flowers for Zelda, with love from her Scottie.'

'Flowers, for me? You should not have gone to all that trouble.' She said. He loved her for saying that because he knew that she sounded pleased. Her happiness meant the world to him. 'Do not be angry with me for not being happier.' He loved her even more, this girl with her perfumed hair.

'Can we steal this warm day, this morning light, this, this what we have right now and run away.'

'But dear, she would say hesitantly. You are not thinking straight now. I have errands to run.' He will argue that love cannot wait. It is impossible for love to wait.

'Stop talking to me as if you are a writer. As if, I am a character in one of your short stories. Scottie, you have neglected me.'

'Well, I am sorry if you feel that I have abandoned you in any way.'

'Have you met someone else? Do I bore you?'

'No. It just happens sometimes in relationships that one person feels neglected and the other is so full of themselves that they forget to pay attention to the people in their environment.'

'It can be the only reason that you have brought me flowers. To apologise for something that is going to happen in the future.'

To this, he had nothing to say and looked out of the window.

'Zelda are you happy here? I am crazy for you dear.'

'I am crazy full stop. Kaput. I know you have a lover. I know you live in Hollywood with her and that she is a gossip columnist.'

'I am not in love with her.'

'You admit it then.'

'You do not have to lay a heavy guilt trip on me.'

'You will learn to love with a passion and a yearning year after year. So, you will learn to love someone else and play by their rules. Their machinations.'

'Just don't write about us.'

'Us. If there even is such a word. Hemingway never liked me.' Zelda said with a pout.

'I drink too much.' Scottie looked out of the window.

'Whose fault is that? You in it for it now. You are in it for the money.'

'What else do you expect me to do Zelda? I need the money. I need to live. I need to eat. I need to put bread on the table.'

'Take me to Paris.'

'Well now, that is out of the question.'

'We were happy there.'

'I would not exactly say that we were happy there. I drank too much. I wasted my talent for years. For years I wasted my literary talent.'

'Golden boy.'

'I will come again.'

'When.'

'I will come again to visit you soon.'

'To bring me more comaed flowers I suppose.'

'I think they brighten up your room.'

'What do you know about anything you alcoholic?'

'Jesus woman. You are terrible.'

'Nobody I know would call me that to my face.'

'Friends. Do you actually have friends, my boy?'

'Yes, in fact I have.'

'Your lover. Is she your 'beautiful little fool' like I once was.'

'Don't cry now.'

'I am not crying fool. Coward. I just sometimes miss 'us'. The way we used to be. I mean I was a socialite once. For God's sake, I was a real somebody and now. Now I am a real nobody.'

'Zelda. We have a child together. A daughter. She misses you like any daughter misses her mother.'

'Does she know I am locked up in here? That I stare day in day out at four walls blankly going quietly insane inside of my head. Am I insane I wonder? Have I just lost touch with reality? Is there a difference husband?'

'I love you Zelda.'

'Don't love me. Stop loving me. Love does me no good in here. I feel so isolated and lonely. Talk to me some more before you go. We have rather splendid memories of the good life, golden boy.'

'Why do you have to call me that?'

'You are nobody special to me anymore. I even call the psychiatric nurse golden. These golden girls. These angels. Do you believe in angels Scottie? What does love have to do with life? I want to keep on living. I promise you this that I want to keep on my living but is it just so damn hard.'

'Have you spoken to the doctors? There are good doctors here.'

'Oh, you mean the psychiatrists. The meanies. Well, I try to explain to them about the voices inside my head and they sit with their pen and notebook in hand. Some take notes and on some days, they hardly bother with me at all. I am crazy Scottie.'

'It does not matter to me if you are or if you are not.'

'Then take me home with you.'

'I can't do that Zelda.'

111

'I love you Scottie.'

'I love you too Zelda.'

'What the dickens is wrong with me? It feels as if my head is buried underground, lights flashing, going on and off, and the craziest things are happening to me. I cannot explain it. Can you explain it to me Scottie?'

'Zelda, it is getting late and you need your rest. Will you eat something before I go? Be a good girl. Eat something before I go.'

'Don't leave me here.'

'I have to. It is for your own good.'

'If you love me, you would not leave me here.'

'I do love you and that is exactly why I am leaving you here. The doctors here will look after you.'

'Sometimes I despise everything and everybody that we ever knew. None of them comes to see me. Am I really such a bad person?

'No. You are a lovely person. You have a smashing personality.'

'You are such an innocent Scottie. If you only knew what happens when you leave. What happens behind these brick walls? I seem to evaporate. Scottie what am I going to do with you? Tell you what. I will keep on loving you even though you are obstinate about the whole thing. Even if you do not love me anymore. That is the thing with crazy. Life will grab you by the hand and tell you to move towards the light, concentrate '

'I am lonely Scottie. Stay with me a while longer. There are too many illiterates in this place. When they ask me if I am married, I say well yes of course I am. When I mention your name, it is as if I have taken out a bazooka and they ask me for real. You are making that up. Then they think that I am the crazy one in that algorithm. I am lonely Scottie. Break me out of here.'

112

'I am lonely too Zelda.'

'I wish we could be together again. A proper family. Kiss me Scottie. I do not care if people are about. They can mind their own business. It is tickets for me anyway. Do you know what I mean by that?'

In his heart F. Scott Fitzgerald knew that many people out there were walking, talking, not saying much about anything idiots. He knew that a lot of them were also well to do alcoholics; some of them were even crazy.

She will be sitting in her room. Always sitting in her room. Waiting for him, forever waiting for him and upon his arrival the conversation would always be the same. He would tell her how much he loved her and she would tell him how much she missed him. They would hardly talk about the kid. He knew that. Staring out of the window. It was not that he had always hated the sanitary smell of hospitals. It always reminded him of death or the wards of hell. A good location for a horror flick. He would creep up on her and surprise her. Kiss her on the cheek. Scottie wanted to say that he was falling apart too but men of that age never made disclosures of that kind. I have lost all my confidence I am afraid he wanted to tell her because he thought that she was the only girl in the world who would understand him and not mistake him for a romantic.

He stared at her as if he was looking at her on their wedding day. He felt slightly out of place. Breathing heavily after all those stairs. Still she did not turn around. It was only when he said her name that at last she turned around. He was afraid that she would not remember him. That he would have to say, it is me, darling. Your husband who has come to see you and he soon forgot all the ugliness in the world and how much he needed a drink. He felt so helpless and cold at the same time. As if, he was carrying winter in his pockets. He wanted to leave. That was his first instinct but she looked so happy to see him. It crushed his heart to see her like this but what could he do under the circumstances. This was the best place for her. I like this weather. He heard himself say from far away. The stars in the city miss you. I do not miss that city for the entire world she replied.

He still felt a kind of passion for her. He blinked back the tears in his eyes. To Scottie this was just a parallel life like when rain meets the pavements, drenches them with liquid and when the liquid mixed with the dust and the rotten dirt of the streets it turned into mud. You smell like champagne Scottie. Sometimes I think that you are too tender with me Scottie. She did not talk about the separation. Thank goodness for that. Are you happy my dear, the words were on his tongue. Of course, I am happy. I am with you am I not. You promised me diamonds. Where are they? There was a choke in his throat. He coughed. Oh, I will bring with me the next time I come. You are such a liar Scottie. You would not have come without a gift. I promise. Next time. She changed then and stared out the window again. Her wanted her to come life again as she had before.

It was always 'Scottie this' and 'Scottie that'. Bright moths seemed to whisper, whisper, and whisper her name at night. The nights in his bedroom in Hollywood. You are my dream girl Zelda, is all that Scottie wanted to say to her when she was like this in the hospital. You are just a ghost story. You are good at making up stories but what is the

114

use of stories? What is the use of it all if there is not any truth in it? I love your stories Scottie because they are so fresh and when you write about girls, I can see that you are writing about me. Sometimes I think I am illusion. Am I an illusion to you Scottie? 'Dream girl', I like those words. Scottie would smile at her, feeling young at heart. Feeling lighthearted. You are careless sometimes Scottie. I do not know why you have to be so careless with my heart sometimes because you know that you are the only one who will ever have access to it.

Scottie sat back in the chair and looked at his wife. Really looked at her. Just do not drink yourself to death friend because then you will be a real loser and all your great talent will be wasted. That was something along the lines of what Hemingway said. In addition to that, Hemingway also said that his wife was insane and they just did not get on. All he could think about was how much he loved her but if he took her in his arms, he would not or could not let go of her and he would see the confusion in her eyes. She would tell him not to remember her like this. To remember her as a socialite, golden boy. He knew that loneliness was just a word. Writers were wed to that word. Their hearts threaded to every catalyst in those letters. He was feeling lukewarm. Scottie felt as if nothing could touch him and Zelda in that moment but he felt he still needed a stiff drink. There is a game in music. Scottie knew Zelda's games. Zelda knew his.

'Do you remember pursuing me Scottie?'
    'Of course I do.'
    'I wish that I was not so sentimental. What you do writer folk call it? You call it by another name.'
    'Is nostalgia the name you are looking for Zelda?'

'Yes, nostalgia. Nostalgia it is.'

'You loved me to death I am afraid Scottie and now it is too late. I can never be a girl again and you can never be that boy again.'

'What do you mean by that Zelda? People fall in love all the time.' Scottie could see that her thoughts were far away.

Mmap Fiction and Drama Series

If you have enjoyed *The Sylvia Plath Effect*, consider these other fine books in **Mmap Fiction and Drama Series** from *Mwanaka Media and Publishing:*

The Water Cycle by Andrew Nyongesa
A Conversation..., A Contact by Tendai Rinos Mwanaka
A Dark Energy by Tendai Rinos Mwanaka
Keys in the River: New and Collected Stories by Tendai Rinos Mwanaka
How The Twins Grew Up/Makurire Akaita Mapatya by Milutin Djurickovic and Tendai Rinos Mwanaka
White Man Walking by John Eppel
The Big Noise and Other Noises by Christopher Kudyahakudadirwe
Tiny Human Protection Agency by Megan Landman
Ashes by Ken Weene and Umar O. Abdul
Notes From A Modern Chimurenga: Collected Struggle Stories by Tendai Rinos Mwanaka
Another Chance by Chinweike Ofodile
Pano Chalo/Frawn of the Great by Stephen Mpashi, translated by Austin Kaluba
Kumafulatsi by Wonder Guchu
The Policeman Also Dies and Other Plays by Solomon A. Awuzie
Fragmented Lives by Imali J Abala
In the Beyond by Talent Madhuku
Zororo Risina Zororo by Oscar Gwiriri
Sword of Vengeance by Olatubosun David
Finding A Way Home by Tendai Mwanaka

Your Epistle by Solomon A Awuzie
The Restless Run and Ruin of the Roaches and Rats by McLayode
The Reign of Terror by Ntando Gerald
Ibala Lyabwina Nama by Austin Kaluba
Daddy, Please Don't Kill Mama by Natisha Parsons
Pilate's Angels by Goodenough Mashego
Blue threads and other stories by Matthew Kunashe Chikono

Soon to be released

Conversation with my Mother by Wonder Guchu

https://facebook.com/MwanakaMediaAndPublishing/

www.ingramcontent.com/pod-product-compliance
Lightning Source LLC
Chambersburg PA
CBHW050350030726
47503CB00008B/2707